LITTLE HENRY

THE STOLEN CHILD

[A reprint of The Lost Child, 1830]

Timothy Flint

LITERATURE HOUSE / GREGG PRESS
Upper Saddle River, N. J.

Republished in 1970 by
LITERATURE HOUSE
an imprint of The Gregg Press
121 Pleasant Avenue
Upper Saddle River, N. J. 07458

Standard Book Number–8398-0558-6
Library of Congress Card–73-104452

Printed in United States of America

LITTLE HENRY,

THE

STOLEN CHILD:

A NARRATIVE OF FACT.

BY THE LATE REV. TIMOTHY FLINT.

NEW-YORK:

L. COLBY AND COMPANY,

122 Nassau-Street.

1847.

NOTE.

—

THE following Narrative was written several years since, soon after the incidents occurred. Its appearance at this time, it is believed, will be acceptable to the public, and its pages perused with interest and profit. The narrative being interspersed with appropriate religious reflections, will be found well adapted for Juvenile and Sabbath School Libraries.

THE STOLEN CHILD.

———◆———

CHAPTER I.

"In Rama was there a voice heard, lamentation, and weeping, and great mourning, Rachel weeping for her children, and would not be comforted, because they are not."

My young readers may not understand, why, in the following story, I use not the real names of the stolen child, the parents, and the parties concerned. But they may be assured that the chief facts related in it are substantially true. Most of them appeared in the newspapers, especially those near where the child was stolen away. The writer of this narrative conversed with men of the first respectability, who witnessed most of the events here recorded. Hundreds can tell, that, except in some minor points, this story is founded in the most harrowing

1

truth. All that a child, though one of more than common intelligence and brightness, could not tell of his wanderings and sufferings, of a period between two and three years, must necessarily be gathered from the narratives of others, and the circumstances of the case as explained by the account of the child after his return to his parents.

Before I begin to relate my story, I wish to apprize my young readers that my principal object in doing it is to soften, as far as I may, their young hearts to pity and all good feelings. I wish to impress upon them, that parents, who are really religious and devout, have strong consolation in deep affliction from trust in God and from the filial confidence with which they draw near to Him in prayer. I wish, also, to prove to religious parents, that when their children, whom they have consecrated to God, are separated from them by distance, and exposed to sickness and dangers by sea, or by land, or that even when these dear ones are taken from them by death, the God, who is every where, filling all space, watching all things and beings, has them as much in hi

hand, and in his holy keeping, as when the
parents have covered them in their winter
beds, and left them to quiet slumber, through
a night of cold and howling winds and
storms.

The parents of the lost child were children of respectable planters in a southern
state, it is believed of the Methodist persuasion. When they were in the freshness of
their youth. they saw, loved each other, and
were married. Instead of settling down with
small means, in an old and thickly settled
country, they felt the vigor and sanguine
confidence of youth, impelling them to go
far away to the south-western country, near
the frontiers of New Mexico, where some of
their neighbors had already removed, and
gave a flattering account of the country and
its advantages.

The year after their marriage they began
this long journey. They crossed through
" the nations," as the southern people call
them; that is to say, they travelled through
the territories of the Creek and Chickasaw
Indians. Here they saw white people, who
were quite as wild as the Indians; and

wretched white men, who, because of their bad hearts and actions, had become outlaws and married Indian women; miserable white women who were married to savage men, runaway negroes, and a variety of sights to inspire sober people, who had never been far from their own pleasant and happy homes before, with feelings of home-sickness. But this young pair were in full health and in innocence; strong in love for each other, and, more than all, fortified with the fear of God; and they were enabled to overcome this feeling as it arose in their bosoms. They dreamed of their distant home, and of the church filled with familiar and kind faces, and of their holidays spent in gentle and innocent gaiety, when they laid them down at night among these rude and fierce looking copper-colored beings; and their hearts at times sunk within them, as they heard wicked words and horrid oaths uttered around them. Then they said to each other, God is every where. We can find a temple under every tree. Every wild bird sings his praises. If we meet no one to love abroad, we will love each other more tenderly. Let

us on to our purpose towards the setting
sun; and when we arrive at our resting
place we will create a peaceful and happy
home, and God, our Father, will look down
upon us and bless us in the wilderness.

So fortified, this pair plunged deeper and
deeper in the forests, until from the heights
of Memphis, they looked down upon the
broad and deep Mississippi, rolling below
them. They crossed this wild and turbid
stream, and made their way through the
cotton-wood and Peccan forests, west of that
river, to the Arkansas. It was in the Autumn. The river was low. They admired
its wide and clean sand bars, and the deep
tangle of vines and tall cane on its banks.
Their way had been for the most part
through woods and prairies. They now
came upon deep cypress swamps and frequent bayous. They often saw bears, and
towards sunset heard the angry cry of the
panther, not unlike the creaking of an un-
oiled carriage wheel when heavily laden.
When night closed in around them, hundreds of owls hooted from the trees. The
wolves howled as they scented their dogs

1*

and horses. Myriads of musquitoes swarmed in their faces, and by the very sound of their wings created a feeling of fever. How strange it is that such young people will leave the place where they were born and reared, and all the comforts of social life, thus to roam away into the depths of the wilderness. Yet, if God had not inspired this disposition to roam, and this curiosity to see new countries, and this courage to encounter difficulties such as these, people would multiply about the paternal house, until there would be neither space nor food for them. Unless multitudes who felt and acted from this spirit of enterprise and endurance, had faced the dangers of entering unknown forests, the savages, wild beasts and musquitoes, where would have been our great and populous country, spreading beyond the lakes and towards the setting sun?

Not to mention the incidents of their journey, as it would prolong my story, they crossed the Arkansas, ascended it three hundred miles,—left its waters and went seventy or eighty miles in a straight direction

from them, and towards Little Washita, a
stream that empties into the Washita, and
on which lies a singular country called
"Mount Prairie." On this large hill of land
of inky blackness, affording space for some
hundred farms, they chose a tract of ground
and purchased it of the government. It
was half prairie, half wood-land, exceeding-
ly fertile and covered on the surface with
large sea shells, although it was more than
three hundred miles from the nearest point
of the sea. Here on a charming spot on
the prairie, just on the verge of a forest of
Peccans and white walnuts, overrun by
wild grape vines, but as clear of underbrush
as an orchard, they built a comfortable log-
house and quarters for four or five black
domestics whom they had brought from
their parents, and who loved their young
master and mistress in humility inspired by
their condition, but with the strong affection
that brothers and sisters feel for each other.
They built also, a barn, a corn-house, a
smoke-house, and a spring-house over a
beautiful spring that flowed down a slope
of the hill. The next thing was to fence

their ground. All the settlements of our great and happy country began in this way; and however rough and unlike the fine houses of towns they may seem, they are often very comfortable; even more so than houses where there is more show, fashion and pride. When any one feels inclined to despise such plain and coarse beginnings, it should be remembered that it is to them we owe the present prosperity and cultivation that surround us.

They soon "opened," as the phrase is, a fine field, and began the pleasant and important process of tilling it. Neighbors settled about them, and it was a pleasant sight in the bright mornings to see the smokes of the new settlers rising above the trees and streaming over the prairie. It was a pleasant sound to hear the chanticleer in the yards under the green trees, or the dogs baying in the woods, seeming as though they liked to hear their own joyous sounds repeated by the echoes.

Some of their neighbors were like themselves, quiet, domestic and disposed to be religious. Others who had fled from debt, a bad name, or a guilty conscience, were no addition either to the comfort or advantage of the settlement. But this affectionate and good couple talked over by themselves the course which they ought and intended to pursue, and took counsel to study the characters of their neighbors, that they might know with whom to associate on terms of intimacy, with whom to be civil, and with whom to preserve a decent but a cautious distance. As soon as the nature of the case would admit, they began to consult with their seriously disposed neighbors about the importance of inviting some of the itinerant ministers to come among them. The husband was the first man in the settlement to assemble people and prepare one of those rude but comfortable wilderness-places of worship, in which God has, perhaps, been as acceptably worshipped as in temples of marble columns and gilding.

It was not long before there were a hundred farms on Mount Prairie and around it. There are few places in the world more remarkable for beauty and pleasantness of situation.

On one side this noble hill swelled from the south and opened a wide view of prairies, copses and woodlands for a great distance towards Great Red River. In the other direction the northern slope looked upon the flint hills which rise on the banks of the Arkansas. On either side might be seen far down upon the plains, flocks of deer bounding away amidst the grass and flowers, or feeding in constant motion, to keep off the swarms of flies that annoyed them. Nature has not formed the country here as in the more thickly inhabited regions of the north. There she has always clothed her wild dominions with thick woods. But in the country of which I am speaking, there are level grass plains like the most beautiful hay fields of the northern country. Intermixed with copses and woodlands, these plains stretch away a thousand miles in extent from Mount Prairie. The parents of the stolen child soon had a fine farm. Their hundred cattle fed in the adjacent plains. They were surrounded by abundance, and every thing upon which they laid their hands seemed to prosper. And well it might be so—for they lived in love and peace. Their house was a place from which arose from pure and humble hearts, devout prayers and thanks-givings to the Author of all good; and what was more, they lived as they prayed, a life of industry and innocence, in the constant discharge of their duty—abstaining from evil speaking and slander, and striving to make peace when there were quarrels and heart-burnings among the uncultivated people around them.

In the course of a few years, this amiable family had obtained as the reward of their industry, sobriety and good conduct, an am-ple portion of the good things of this world. Their cotton fields and their flocks afforded them clothing. A hundred kine gave them an abundance of milk, and the wild woods yielded them honey from the numerous swarms of bees that live in the hollow trees of these forests, in such quantities that they might be said to "flow in milk and honey." Out of every little copse about the house would start away droves of hares. Squir-rels by hundreds played in the Peccan trees that stood around. In the winter, countless numbers of geese and swans and sand-hill cranes and pelicans and other majestic and beautiful water-fowls came from the frozen countries and the immense lakes of the north to feed upon the acorns, nuts and seeds that are to be found in the woods and prairies throughout the mild winter of this climate. They begin to arrive as soon as the middle or end of October. This is the season of Indian summer, as it is called in the country of which I speak; and a pleasant season it is. The leaves of the trees have just turned to such bright red, brown, yellow and orange colors, with here and there a little deep green, and are beginning to fall. The heat of the sun is tempered to a mild warmth, and he rises broadened in the morning from behind a bank of crimson mist and sinks into one at night. The hazel bushes are weighed down with their fine ripe nuts. Sweet wild grapes hang in clusters from vines of great size which spread over many of the trees. The persimon touched by the first frost, is delicious, and amply repays the trouble of climbing the high trees upon which it grows. The paw-paw, too, in its rich yellow lies every where upon the ground. The rabbits and squirrels dart about through the dry and falling leaves. During the whole of this happy time, flights of migrating birds are heard uttering their strange notes high up in the air. To those who have associated in their minds the croaking noise which they make with this delightful period, it is an agreeable sound.

In the cold and stormy days, for there are some such even here, the little ponds and water courses are covered with them; and when their wings are heavy with sleet, whole flocks can be taken with little trouble, and they are sometimes domesticated in the farm yards. Thus passed the years of this family in peace, and love, and innocent enjoyment. Beautiful birds sang for them at morning and evening, and they were satisfied with their home, though it was more than a thousand miles from the place where they were born. Three fine children were born to them in succession. These blessings sent from God, united their hearts more tenderly in the dear bonds of domestic affection. To their prayers was now added an earnest desire that God would strengthen them to be faithful to the great duty of attempting to bring up these beloved ones in the love and fear of Him; and as "a seed to seek, and a generation to serve Him." They discoursed often and earnestly together how they should rear their children to be good and know their duty and acquire useful learning; and how they should always walk before them in a discreet and Christian example. Nor did they cease to ask of God, that their children might have kind and affectionate dispositions of heart, and such minds that they might be trained to be respectable and useful.

I am led to believe, that the subject of this narrative was born in the year 1820. Henry Howe was a beautiful child in infancy; and as he grew in years, he grew in beauty. But, what was infinitely more important, he was intelligent and engaging in manner, of an amiable disposition, and affectionate to his parents, and brother and sister. The first manifestations of his mind and heart were alike favorable to both his heart and mind. His parents deemed him of more than common promise; and with delighted affection, watched the first dawnings of his character. When little Henry had reached the age of four years, his beauty and affectionate conduct to those around him, attracted the general attention of the neighbors. His parents had already taught him several little hymns, which he would repeat with a strength of memory and a distinctness and sweetness of voice, as surprising to every one, as it was gratifying to the fond pride of these good parents.

Unfortunately, the quickness of mind displayed by this fine boy, began to call forth a sinful weakness in the too fond parents. They evidenced this by frequent praises of the little Henry, which escaped them almost unknown to themselves. They seldom had the neighbors come in to spend the evening with them, without showing how constantly their minds dwelt upon the uncommon smartness of the little fellow. He was called upon to recite his hymns, answer his questions, and in other ways display his

knowledge. Repeated manifestations of this
kind of folly excited ill will in the minds of
those parents about them, who were natur-
ally inclined to envy. They thought of
their own less gifted, less amiable, and less
instructed children, and either hated or
laughed at these parents. Even the brother
and sister of little Henry, had they not been
good, like him, might have seen and felt the
partial attention bestowed upon the beloved
boy. Nothing can be more injurious, unjust
or ruinous, than such mistakes in parents. I
must say, however, in excuse of this instance
of such folly, that the parents did it in general unconsciously, and were not aware of
the extent to which they carried their favor-
itism. Their hearts, full of parental love,
only overflowed too strongly in one direction.

Bitterly were these parents punished for
this injudicious and unjust fondness. I do
not say as some, who are good men notwithstanding, would say, that they were punished by heaven for making this child an idol,
and loving him more than their other children and their God. And yet I know not
when parents really allow their love for

their children to run to a foolish and sinful excess, beyond what reason or religion authorise, why God may not justly punish such a fondness by taking away the idol to which their hearts are joined, and causing them to stand corrected by leaving them nothing but himself to love.

Certain it is, that whatever was the purpose of a gracious and righteous Providence, a train of events was going on which was shortly to deprive them of this idol of their affections. Not only had this almost boastful love for little Henry, with the child's real superiority, stirred the bad feelings of some of the wicked spirits of the settlement, but they envied his growing wealth and hated to see his flocks and herds spread upon the plains. Their hearts burned with anger to remark his good children taking the first places at school. Added to all this, Mr. Howe was spoken of as delegate to the legislative assembly. What bitterness they felt, when, as was often the case, they heard him praised; for nothing so surely stirs the venom of bad hearts as to hear the deserved praises of others. O! my dear young

2*

friends, what a horrible feeling that must
be, which can thus fill and blacken the
heart, until it becomes like that of a fiend
and hates to see and hear of good and
happiness.

But, more than all, these people hated
Mr. Howe on account of his example; so
unlike theirs, which constantly showed them
as in a glass, their own deformed likeness;
and for his having the courage to set his
face resolutely against swearing, and drink-
ing, and horse-racing, and against hunting,
firing at a mark, or gambling on the Sabbath. They hated him, in short, for the
firmness with which he opposed evil-doers
of all descriptions and of every character.
He was always in readiness to step forward
and aid in breaking up the combinations of
negro-stealers, gamblers, horse-thieves and
desperadoes of a still darker character;
whose members sometimes lurked in and
around the settlement. When an outrage
was committed the perpetrators fled beyond
the bounds of our country, to the adjacent
Mexican province of Texas. It was a dan-
gerous undertaking to follow such people

to their strong holds in the midst of almost
impenetrable swamps and forests, frequented
by fierce wild beasts, and the chosen abode
of hissing and horribly hideous and venom-
ous snakes. Mrs. Howe often endeavored
to dissuade her husband from these hazar-
dous enterprises. She would tell him that
it was useless to attempt to stop the career
of these desperadoes until it was done by
the strong arm of the law; and that he en-
dangered his life and wasted his strength,
and incurred enmity to no purpose.

He answered, that he felt it to be the duty
of every honest man to exert himself to put
down wickedness and crime wherever they
were to be found; instead of saying to himself, I care not if my neighbor is murdered
or plundered, so long as I am safe. This
conduct as I have said, created in the minds
of some of his neighbors a strong feeling of
enmity towards him; not that they were directly interested in the guilty transactions
which occasionally took place; but the people by whom they were performed, sometimes sojourned among them to spend their
money. They were amused, too. with the

noisy laughter and jollity, and the wild stories of these reckless men, and loved to play
cards with them. There was something so
much like fellow feeling between these fam-
ilies and their guests, that the unwillingness,
which they felt, that any measures should
be taken to ferret out and bring to punishment these prowling disturbers of society,
was very natural.

It would seem that even at the extremest
verge of our Christian country, such facts
could not exist; but it is a truth, that here
were numbers of outlawed wretches, who
had associated themselves together and or-
ganized bands who were ready to commit
any crimes, from a trifling theft to the most
horrible murder. Among them, the only
one which is connected with this story is
the band of negro-stealers, as they are called
in the Southern country. The band, or
gang, extends itself from the slave states to
the free states, and from the North to the
South. They will inveigle a free negro
away with them and transport him to a distant part of the slave-country; and then
forge papers of conveyance and sell him as
a slave.

By promising slaves their freedom, they
induce many to leave a master, who perhaps
is kind, only after travelling a few hundred
miles to be disposed of to one who is cruel.
Others are taken by force. I have heard
the relations of several who were stolen
when they were children. They told of
being hidden in hollow trees for days and
nights; of travelling on foot through wilder-
nesses and feeding upon berries and such
wild fruits as they could find; of sleeping at
night upon the bare ground without the
slightest covering; of being cruelly treated,
when they were found to be not so valuable
as the negro-stealers had supposed them; and
a hundred other circumstances of suffering
which I have not room to mention. It must
be hard for the simple and single minded negro, who has grown up in the family of a
good master to whom he is attached, until he
has taken possession of the piece of ground
and cabin which are henceforth to be his
own, and where he spends his intervals of
rest, surrounded by his wife and children and
in the midst of humble comfort procured by
his own indusrty and good conduct, to be

forced away from it all and to be sold among strangers.

Two wretches belonging to the band of which I have been speaking, who had been particularly active in transactions of this kind, were sojourning at the house of a neighbor of Mr. Howe about the time that little Henry was four years and a half old. Their names were Tuttell and Callendar. The man in whose house they sojourned was unfriendly to Mr. Howe. Many a time had these negro-thieves, as they drank their whiskey at the midnight carousals, uttered shouts of coarse laughter with him as he ridiculed Mr. Howe's religion and his pride in little Henry, and joined in his curses as he talked of the energy and industry with which this hated neighbor pursued their brother desperadoes.

It happened one evening, as they were slandering him in the customary strain, and wishing him no good, that one of them mentioned that he had once been the master of Cæsar, a very industrious, faithful and valuable black servant, belonging to Mr. Howe. A pleasant thought seemed to enter the mind of this bad neighbor, for his countenance brightened. At last he said, "can you procure me evidence that you are now the rightful owner of the man? I will vex Mr. Howe and get money out of him, if I do not frighten him to give up the negro."

The plan was soon settled. Tuttell had actually owned Cæsar for a few months in Georgia, and was able to make out rather a plausible claim to him, which he conveyed with all the necessary formality to this man. The negro-thieves went their way, leaving the malignant neighbor to exult in the meditation that he had now an opportunity to torment Mr. Howe; and it may be, thought he, that I can deprive him of the services of Cæsar, who pretends to love his hypocritical master so much that he would never willingly live with another.

Accordingly he soon called upon Mr. Howe and stated the grounds of his claim, requesting him either to give up the negro, or to pay a stipulated price; for such are the phrases in which this unhappy traffic is conducted.

Mr. Howe at first manifested some astonishment at this unexpected demand, believing as he did, that his title to Cæsar was perfectly honest and just, according to the usages of the country. But as soon as he had read the title papers, transferred by Tuttell, he understood the business, and saw at once that it was a deep laid plan to defraud, or intimidate him out of his right. He considered a few moments, and then answered the man calmly, "that he was willing to do justice, as far as he knew it; but that he did not comprehend this matter, and did not believe the claim brought forward a just one; that he knew well the circumstances of the purchase of Cæsar, and that, in short, although he disliked to contend in the law, he would do it rather than give up this servant; as, independent of his value, he was strongly attached to him." Upon this the man began alternately to coax and threaten. Finding, however, that both these measures were unavailing and that he could produce no effect, he departed with an additional infusion of bitterness, united with his former envy, hatred and ill will towards Mr. Howe.

Shortly after this, Tuttell and Callendar returned from Texas, when this man related to them the failure of his attempt. They were all heated with drink and exasperated by this and other recent instances of ill success. In the midst of threats, blasphemies and schemes of revenge, they finally fixed upon the diabolical project, the execution of which I am about to relate.

It was agreed that Tuttell should visit Mr. Howe and urge the unjust claim anew. Should he fail in extorting from him a supply of money to meet his urgent necessities, he took a horrible oath that he would be revenged in some other way. Meanwhile Mr. Howe was informed that this neighbor had been heard to hint darkly at some dreadful event that was shortly to befall him; but he disregarded this information, and when Tuttell called upon him, in pursuance of the plan laid by these fiends in human shape, he received him as calmly as he had done his neighbor. Tuttell explained all the circumstances of the chain of title to Cæsar which he had conveyed to the neighbor with so much ingenuity, plausibility and seeming

3

integrity of intention, that it would have appeared to a common observer that he was himself fully convinced that his representations were true and just. So artfully did he frame his story, that Mr. Howe's convictions upon the subject would have been shaken, had he not known all the circumstances of his servant's former servitude, and consequently felt assured that it was all fiction and forgery.

This conference resulted as the former had done, in the declaration of Mr. Howe, that he would do nothing in the case any farther than he was compelled to do by law. With a countenance lowering with revenge, and smothered threats of vengeance, Tuttell left him.

The three villains now met in conclave again, and devised the plot in which their fiendish purpose should be executed. They took the most dreadful oaths that each would act his own part in the tragedy, and never under any circumstances disclose the slightest point that might furnish any clue to a discovery.

The next morning came in all the brightness of early autumn. The family of Mr. Howe had breakfasted, and as it was Saturday little Henry, now near five years old, looked forward to a day of holiday from school and enjoyment at home. Unaccompanied by his brother and sister, as the walk was thought too long for their little steps, he went with the faithful Cæsar to a spot in the woods where there were hazel nuts and grapes, fruits of which this child, like most others of his years, was fond. Cæsar moved off some distance from him to attend to the felling of some trees, thinking that the little fellow was perfectly safe. He was busily engaged, when he heard the trampling of horses, followed immediately by the scream of a child. As he sped to the spot where he had left little Henry, he heard the loved boy calling upon him in tones of distress and terror. He reached the place just in time to see two men on horseback going off at full gallop, one of whom carried little Henry before him, holding his mouth with his hand to stifle his cries.

In an agony of terror Cæsar ran after them and calling on them to bring the boy back, not believing however that they intended any thing more than to frighten the child, and have a wretched frolic of that sort. He thought that after they had satisfied their malignant natures with this sport, they would either set him down or bring him back. But Cæsar followed them at his full speed in vain, for they rapidly gained upon him, and he saw them passing over the prairie and disappearing in the distant woods without manifesting any purpose to conclude the mischievous and cruel frolic by returning the child.

He was now two miles from home and exhausted with fatigue and distress of mind. Sensible of the folly of attempting to follow any farther on foot and alone, his next thought was to return to the house of his master and have the wretches instantly pursued. He retraced his steps with the utmost rapidity that he could command; but when he came in sight of his hitherto happy dwelling, the heart of the faithful and affectionate creature died within him. How could he tell the sad tale of this cherished child, the lovely and intelligent and affectionate favorite of the whole household, being lost to them? Taken away too, in such a manner! He must stand the charge of carelessness and neglect of his duty, which he knew would be made against him, after the first burst of sorrow had passed and the parents had time to meditate upon their misery.

But he never for a moment thought as a bad servant would have done, of concealing the fact and leaving it to come out by the observed absence of the child. He rushed into the presence of the parents, and with a countenance which exhaustion and the agony of conflicting emotions rendered almost white with paleness, he told his tale of alarm and horror. I leave my young readers to imagine the scene that followed. The mother allowed the tide of agonized feelings to overcome her, and she fainted. The father when he saw her again open her eyes upon life and misery, snatched his pistols and ran for his horse.

A good neighbor coming up on horseback at the time, offered to accompany the agonized father as soon as any one had calm-

3*

ness enough to inform him what had happened. In a few minutes they were both in full pursuit in the direction in which the child was carried off. The uncontrollable feelings of Mr. Howe would have induced him to have ridden his horse down in an hour; but his calmer friend, by gentle advice and persuasion, made him sensible that this was not the right calculation, for if it was nothing more than a malicious frolic played off to frighten Mr. Howe, nothing would be gained by such a fierce pursuit; and if it was really the meditated revenge of his enemies, they could not hope to overtake them, except by managing the pursuit more discreetly than the two men did their flight, as they must now be ahead of them a full hour's ride.

Accordingly they proceeded on their way at as great speed as they thought their horses could bear, in silence, only interrupted by the groans and heart-rending exclamations of the father, who saw and acknowledged in the taking away of this favorite child the hand of God, depriving him of the idol which had arisen between him and his

Creator. They passed over one prairie and
then another, the father still straining his
eyes in advance; but no trace was to be
seen of the stolen child. An agonizing circumstance now occurred. They had
reached a point where the road branched
off in three directions. One led to the Little Washita; another to Little Rock on the
Arkansas; and a third far to the southwest
on the Kiamesia.

But they were all roads of unfrequent
travel, and little more than cattle traces. As
horses in great numbers were constantly
moving over each, it would seem at the
first thought impossible to determine which
route the two men had taken. It is curious
to note the acuteness of the ways in which
people who live in the new and back countries decide in such a case. By examining
attentively, they can distinguish between the
tracks of various horses that have all passed
over the same road.

The tracks being distinctly impressed
upon the loom, give indications that enable
a practised observer to pronounce instantly
whether the horses had passed on quickly

and borne the weight of a man, or whether
they had walked carelessly as they went on
their way to graze. Mr. Howe and his
neighbor came to the conclusion, after dis-
mounting and looking at the tracks, that the
wicked men had taken the road to Little
Washita. They followed them on this
route until they came to a marsh covered
with water to the horses fetlocks. This
marsh extended each way two miles in
length and was a half of a mile wide. Here
it was impossible for any sagacity to dis-
criminate the route which had been taken
by those of whom they were in pursuit.
The father stopped his horse on the edge of
this marsh, and as all the uncertainty of
what was before them rushed upon him, his
eyes filled with tears. Terrible words of
vengeance rose to his lips, but better feelings came to his relief as he looked towards
heaven and remembered the example of
Him who was led to sufferings and death
by the revenge of his enemies, *as a sheep before her shearers is dumb.*

In imitation of another example from the
book he had chiefly read, he gave utterance

to the feelings of nature. Oh Henry ! the
wretches have made sure work in their vengeance ! *Would to God, I could die for
thee, my son, my son.*

After consulting together, they agreed
each to take a different direction through
the swamp or marsh, and to keep on sepa-
rately three or four miles, inquiring at any
houses that they came in sight of, if the two
men had been seen, when they would meet
again and consult what was best to be done
further. They followed this plan, but neither
heard of the lost child or saw any traces of
the objects of their pursuit. The wretches
had thought too deeply upon their horrid
plan of revenge to allow themselves to be
easily traced, or to be seen by any one.
The father and his neighbor were destitute
of money or food, and every way unpre-
pared for a journey. But it was out of the
question to think of returning to the mother
of little Henry without tidings of him, and
to allow the cruel men to gain still more in
advance of them, and consequently a more
certain chance of escaping from the country
without detection or punishment.

The village at Little Washita, the first which they would see on the route they had taken, was thirty miles distant; though this was the travelled road to Washita county and Great Red River. They determined to make their way thither as fast as possible, and thence despatch people in every direction to aid them in their search. The feelings and thoughts of the father, as he now moved on in the belief that days of the most terrible suspense must pass before he could hope to hear of this loved and lost child, can better be imagined than described. The hope of an immediate discovery was now given up. His kind neighbor endeavored to comfort him; but what relief can be given in such distress apart from the solace of religion.

To deepen the gloom of their situation, clouds gathered thick on the face of the sky. Lightning gleamed above and around, and threw flashes of light upon them, until their eyes were almost blinded. The fierce thunderbolt fell before them, as in a silence of awe they proceeded over a naked prairie. Sheets of rain and hail now began to fall.

The father through all this storm only suffered from the thought, that his little Henry
was probably exposed to the same tempest, without a kind look, or word, to cheer
and sustain his trembling heart; perhaps
cruelly tormented by the wretches, who
would delight in his tears and cries. Poor
little fellow! If my young readers could
picture to themselves the thoughts that
passed through the mind of this dear boy,
as he remembered the soothing and affectionate voice of his mother, as she smoothed
his hair, and kissed his cheek in the morning; and the kind look of his father, as he
used to lay his head to sleep upon his knee
in the evening; and his heart swelled almost to bursting, amidst the " pitiless pelt-
ing" of the storm, as he felt the difference of
his present situation, subjected to bitter
mockery and harsh words, they would determine, as they look around upon a happy
home, in which they dwell, as cherished
things, feel the soft impress of a mother's
kiss, and lay their heads in safety upon a
father's breast, to be good and thankful to
God, and their parents, and never do any

act that might call down upon them such a dreadful reverse, as was the lot of little Henry.

He had lost his hat in attempting to escape from the hands of the man who first seized him. His eyes were swollen with weeping, and the rain drops, that drove in his face, mingled with his tears. His light clothing was soon drenched with wet, and he was faint for want of his customary food. His head ached, and his temples throbbed so painfully, that he would gladly have laid down upon the ground, uncomfortable as the wet earth would have been; but he felt that this would not be allowed him. A feeling of deadly sickness came over him; and a mist seemed to spread before his eyes. He lost the hold which kept him on the horse, and fell to the ground. One of the wretches dismounted and lifted him up, shook him roughly, swore at him, and after setting him up behind his companion, told him to take care how he fell off again. But the other man, perceiving that the child could not keep himself in his seat, unbuckled the leathern belt, from which hung his pis-

tols and knife, and passing it around Henry
and himself, fastened it again. The poor
boy, thus prevented from the danger of falling, went to sleep on horseback from exhaustion and fatigue.

It would only pain and weary my youthful readers, to follow the father of this unfortunate child, and his kind and compas-
sionate neighbor, in a detailed account of
what they endured, through that raging
storm. As I have said, the father's distress
of mind precluded all other suffering. The
neighbor was a hardy backwoodsman, a
hunter used to fatigue and exposure, and
his affection for his own little ones was enlisted strongly in this case. Besides, he
thought Mr. Howe a good man, and felt
deeply interested for him.

The night was now coming on. The
tempest had abated in a degree; but the
sky was still covered with heavy black
clouds. Twilight came, and disappeared,
leaving Mr. Howe and his neighbor surrounded by the thickness of black darkness.
Their fatigued horses refused to be driven
at a pace faster than a walk; and it was

evident to the riders, that they would soon be too much exhausted for even that pace.

Prudence prevailed over blind affection, and Mr. Howe consented to stop at the first dwelling to which they should come, and procure such food for themselves, and refreshment for their horses, as would enable them to proceed on their journey. They made their way along slowly, and without a single ray of light, except from occasional faint gleams of lightning, until they reached a lonely house on the verge of a wood. The owner, though rough in manners, was kind hearted and hospitable. He entered at once into the situation of Mr. Howe. He gave such food as the house could supply ; and instead of simply feeding their worn out horses, he brought them two of his own that were strong and untired. He did still more. He undertook, dark and dreary as the night was, to follow one trace to Little Washita village himself, while he pointed out other routes which the two travellers could take to the same place. Each of the three were to stop at every dwelling on their way, and inquire for the lost child.

The thunder stilll rolled at a distance, and the darkness had not lessened. There were bayous, and pit-falls, and unfordable streams, deep forests and muddy swamps in the way. Yet neither of these men, with such an object, shrunk from the danger or unpleasantness of the undertaking. The three had concluded, that there was some probability in the opinion, that the two men with the child would confide so far in the chances of safety from pursuit, in consequence of the storm in the afternoon and the darkness of the night, as to stop at some house. Mr. Howe and his neighbor still inclined to believe, that this was the direction which they had taken.

While the three friends were thus putting their purpose in execution, let us return to the desolate house, from whence so dearly beloved a child had been taken. A hundred times in the day did the almost distracted mother run to the door, to see if her husband was not returning with Henry in his arms. She would remain for some moments looking down upon the plain, until objects seen through her tears became in fancy such as

she wished to see. The horses, slowly returning before the approaching storm, deceived her again and again. At times her
heart almost leapt from her bosom, as she
thought she actually saw the loved forms
drawing near. But the day wore away,
and one hope after another proved illusive.

The children, depressed by the gloom
and anxiety impressed upon every countenance, and from an undefined feeling of
loneliness and desolation, gathered around
her in tears. No one thought of food. The
servants came in with their dark and length-
ened visages dejected with sorrow and anxiety. To add the last finish to their gloom,
the dark storm came on. Think of this mother's heart, as she thought of her cherished
boy, whom the winds of heaven had not
been allowed to visit too roughly, in all
probability exposed to all the terrors and
dangers of that dreadful evening.

There are many cases of hopeless misery
like this, in the life of every one; and we
have, each one of us for ourselves, to walk
through the darkness of the shadow of death.
What shall sustain us, and how shall we be

able calmly to pass through scenes like these? There is, my dear young friends, but one effectual resource, and it is love, trust and submission to our Heavenly Father. When the storm at length overshadowed this sorrow-stricken dwelling, the whole family, not even excepting the humble but faithful and attached domestics, were assembled around the distressed mother. She opened the Bible. She read of Hagar cast out with Ishmael, and ready to perish in the desert. She read of the providential spring which they saw when the mother had retired apart, that she might not see her little son expire of thirst. She read of the Shunamite widow, to whom her son was restored alive. She read of the widow of Nain, as she received her son from the hands of the Saviour. She read with renewed confidence from the thousand passages of the Scriptures, which speak of the tender mercy and fatherly care of the Almighty, who watcheth over a sparrow's fall, and numbereth even the hairs of the head; and who pitieth the sorrows of his creatures, "even as a father pitieth his children."

4*

She knelt down and prayed before them, that the dear one might be restored to them unhurt; that they might sing together the joyful song, "for this my son was dead, and is alive again; was lost, and is found."

The hearts of the attached servants united with their mistress as she prayed, and their tears flowed less painfully as they thus sought relief. But though they felt that their great sorrow was soothed, and deprived of a portion of its bitterness by this holy exercise, and by the consideration that the strong and the weak, the great and the small, are alike under the care of God, and that his protection and love can be extended alike to all places, and that his hand can alike support and sustain in every variety of trial. It cannot be supposed that any in that dwelling slept through the long and dreary night which followed this heart-rending day.

The mother walked the floor and wept for hours after stillness had come upon every person and thing around her. The low and distant thunder seemed to her excited imagination an unnatural sound, and she felt as though all nature was pervaded with the same deep gloom that weighed upon her mind and heart. But this unfortunate mother knew that the indulgence of such feelings was a weakness, and she struggled against them. She again knelt in prayer, and her earnest cries to God for her child *prevented the mourning.*

The morning dawned equally upon the mother in her grief, and to the pursuers at Little Washita, without bringing any tidings of the lost one to either. The three pursuers had made their way safely through the darkness to the point at which they were to meet; though God only can know what thoughts passed through the father's mind as he slowly traversed the swamps, forests and bayous. Not one of them had heard a word of the wretches. Mr. Howe was wearied, exhausted and almost heart-broken. The cries of the night birds had thrilled upon his ear in the depths of the forest as the expiring wail of his dear Henry.

But he remembered that he had a wife and children, each of whom ought to have been as dear as the one he had lost at home. His friends advised him to despatch persons

from the village in all directions for forty
miles around; and then to return himself to
his home and rally the settlement to search
that quarter thoroughly. He hired a dozen
men to go from the village and saw them
set off. He advertised the wretches every
where in that region by putting up at all
the public places a written statement of the
circumstances of the case, and the offer of a
large reward to any one who should find
the child or give any clue that might lead
to a discovery of him.

Having thus taken every measure that
his own thoughts or the advice of others
suggested, he retraced his sad steps homeward. He arrived there and exchanged sad
and silent embraces with his wife and children, without needing to relate the ill success of his painful journey. It would be
useless for the young reader to endure the
pain of following the father in his laborious
and unremitting efforts to discover the rob-
bers and his child. Little Henry was described and advertised, and a large reward
offered for his discovery in fifty newspapers.

Written statements, such as I have before

mentioned, were posted up in all the conspic-
uous places on the Mississippi towards Washita, Red River and Texas, and in New
Orleans. The country was traversed hundreds of miles in all directions. Even the
villain who had aided in forming the plan of
carrying the child off, joined in the search.
Sometimes the miserable father would listen
to gossip stories which represented that the
child had been seen in one place and in
one set of circumstances, and then in
another. Once he thought that he was actually on a certain train to find his son.
He heard of two men who carried a child
on horseback that was often heard to cry.
He followed the trace three hundred miles,
overtook the men, and found at last that it
was not his Henry, but a child whose father
was removing with him to a distant region
of the country.

Fifty times were they deceived, not ex-
actly in this way, but the disappointments
were all bitterly felt. Oftentimes would
the thoughtless neighbors, not intending
harm relate what they had heard, as that
two bad looking men had been seen by a

spring, first one whipping the child and then the other. They would go into a most afflicting tediousness of narrative in speaking of the screams of the poor little fellow and his paleness as he was seen sitting on a log on the ground. Then they spoke of his growing faint, his cries sinking away; and finally, the wicked and merciless villians were supposed to have despatched him with a knife. How directly these stories all went to the hearts of the parents!

Meantime these parents, from having been remarkable for freshness of countenance, high health and cheerfulness, became pale, bilious and bore dejected and care-worn faces. The father spent most of his time from home in journeys of two or three hundred miles distance, worn with fatigue and carrying upon his sad countenance the impress of deep sorrow at his heart. His concerns at home would have been neglected had not the faithful black servants redoubled their care, exertion and industry in the absence of their master. They tenderly loved the lost Henry, and deeply sympathised with their master and mistress. But it is the nature of these humble and affectionate beings not to remember their sorrows as long as do the people of the white race. Besides, they felt that they could in no way manifest their pity so sincerely, as by being faithful to their master's interest and taking good care of his plantation in his absence.

There are a great many parents who can imagine the mental suffering which Mr. Howe endured as he journied first to one distant place and then to another, always describing his little Henry and plying all that he met with questions whether they had seen or heard any thing of him. Some people, with kind intentions, sent him off in this direction, and others with indifferent and careless hardness of heart, prophesied, merely to show that they were wise men and prophets, that the child would be found in a particular place; and the half distracted father, to leave nothing undone, posted away in that direction.

But it was natural that in such a heart-wearing search, experiencing constant disappointment, he should at length get discouraged and listen with impatience and almost with fretfulness to these vague and gossip rumors. What must have been the feelings of the mother during the long absence of her husband, always returning the same sad answer, "no news"? What a shiver it brought to her heart as in the dark and dreary winter night she heard the wolves howl in the far plains and the storm sweep through the leafless limbs of the trees! Sometimes the children would awaken all the strength of her sorrow by asking, "Mamma, where do you think poor brother Henry is?"

Oh how her blood chilled in her veins to believe that he was in the hands of such cruel men, she knew not where, nor how. Full thankfully would she have heard that he was dead, that he was released from their iron hands, and his bones decently covered up under the soil. Her thoughts would wander. Her imagination would paint. Sometimes she saw him as her gossiping neighbors told their tale, pale, wan, his fair locks dishevelled, his little hands folded as he implored them to spare him when they came upon him with the uplifted knife, after having cruelly beaten him with rods. Sometimes she imagined she saw a wolf or a panther springing upon him, or saw him roasted alive by the Indians. In her dreams she suffered still acuter misery. She fancied herself wandering alone in the wild woods. Far off and half seen in the darkness she saw the figure of Henry flitting away from her. Then the mother would arise in her heart. She would spring from her bed and in attempting to grasp the dear shade, would awaken herself to solitude and misery. She never saw the other children seated around the table for their food without being reminded of the dear one that was wanting. God only can count the tears which this affectionate mother shed.

But when she saw her sorrowing husband returning from his long and disheartening journies, pale, and wan, and discouraged, she felt a noble purpose to check and conceal her own maternal sorrows and make.an effort to comfort him. Religion, as it ought, spoke at length to their hearts and descended in its peaceful influences upon their spirits, like dew upon the thirsty sands of the des-

5

ert. They saw that God had spared to
them two other children, good, intelligent
and lovely. They knew that it was the order of things every where in this world of
sorrow and death, that God should take
away children from parents by the stroke
of death; and that religion calls upon the
sufferers in such cases to bow their head to
the stroke of the Almighty, and to say, *it is
the Lord; though he slay me, yet will I trust
in him.* They, therefore, wrestled with
God, that he would cause them to believe
and to feel, that the dear child was taken
away and had gone to Him, and was with the
little ones in Heaven, of whom the Saviour
declared the kingdom of Heaven consists.

Though these parents thus endeavored to
subdue the anxiety and distress which
preyed upon their health and almost bowed
them to the earth, and though repeated disappointments had nearly extinguished hope
within them, yet there was still always
enough of excitement and even hope in their
minds, to keep the father and mother, and **I**
may add the children too, in a state of constant and harrowing anxiety.

At this period, which was about a year from the time when the child was lost, a neighbor came in one morning and told them that he thought he could at last give them some certain information touching the fate of their lost child. From the countenance of the man as he said this, they could gather nothing with regard to the nature of the news. He seemed to have an air of mystery and would say nothing in the presence of the family ; but informed the father that if he would accompany him to a certain place he thought he could set his mind at rest as to the fate of his child.

The father and mother instantly inferred that the man supposed the child to be dead, although he did not say so. How strangely blinded we are to what passes in our own minds ! This mother had often thought and said that she should be glad if she was sure her dear Henry had escaped from the hands of cruel men and was safe in the presence of God in a better world. But when she first felt as though her wishes had been heard and granted, and that her poor Henry was actually dead, the grief of a mother rose within her and she fainted. As soon as she recovered, her husband mounted his horse and accompanied his neighbor.

He led him in silence along the road where the child had last been seen, until they were about a mile beyond the point where the child had passed from the view of Cæsar, when he turned off into a deep ravine, covered on every side with thick vines and brier bushes. A spring ran along the bottom of it. It was a dark, dreary and out of the way place, surrounded by thick woods, and the very spot where bad men would have chosen to perpetrate a deed of horror.

Here the man stopped and dismounted. The father followed him in anxious silence. At a little distance from the source of the spring beside a log, were bones such as the imperfect knowledge which Mr. Howe had of the structure and the anatomy of the human body, might lead him to suppose were those of a child. They were laid a little disordered, as by some beast that had carelessly walked over them. But there were apparently the chief bones of the little body.

There was the skull, and to make the evidence more complete, locks of fair hair, such as those which covered the head of Henry, were scattered around. The neighbor said but little; and little was necessary to bring home the conviction to the heart of this unfortunate parent, that here his dear child had perished, and that this was all that remained of him. It is useless to attempt to describe how he felt. The bones were carefully carried to his house. A good Methodist minister prayed, sang a funeral hymn and preached a sermon, and then the bones were interred as those of Henry. There were few dry eyes in this funeral meeting, as the minister in the simple pathos of truth spoke of the pathetic circumstances of the case. The mother saw the bones buried beneath the soil; but she retained the fair locks, one of which she wore next her bosom, and her eye was often seen to fill with unbidden tears, and often towards the close of the day she strayed alone to the spot where she deemed that all of the child that was mortal was at rest.

5*

CHAPTER II.

'God is the father of the orphan.'

Let me now call the attention of my youthful reader to the stolen child. I have said that at the time he was carried away, he was near five years old, and of a quickness, intelligence and strength of judgment beyond his years. He had seen Tuttell at his father's house, and when the men on horseback approached the spot where he was picking nuts, he immediately recognized him as one of them. It was Tuttell that seized him and placed him on horseback before himself, while his companion threatened the little fellow with instant death if he did not cease his cries. They set off at full gallop, Tuttell endeavoring all the time to stop his screams by covering his mouth with his hand. Little Henry was obliged to struggle hard to get an opportu-

nity to tell Tuttell that he knew well that
he could not get away, and that he would
promise if they would leave his mouth un-
covered, not to make any more noise, but
remain entirely silent. In relating the conversations of these men with the child and
each other, I shall omit altogether all their
curses. I shall omit the horrid words in
which every few minutes they asked God
to punish them by destroying their souls.

"Do you hear," said one to the other,
"how the little hypocrite talks already?
Preaching runs in the blood of the family.
Can you preach good, my little man?"

Henry with a prudence and sagacity beyond his years, saw at once that remon-
strance and complaint would be unavailing
but would even aggravate his hard case,
and he determined neither to complain nor
talk at all, unless it seemed absolutely necessary.

The men continued to gallop on with him
farther and still farther, amusing themselves
meanwhile in picturing the confusion and
distress into which this event would throw
the quiet and well regulated family of Mr.

Howe, or the canting hypocrite, as with many curses they called him.

The heart of the poor little fellow died within him as he looked back and saw the hill and the woods of his father's house disappear, and he ventured to ask them how far they were going to carry him and what they meant to do with him?

"What do we mean to do with you?" said Tuttell with a strong brogue, for he was an Irishman. "May be we will have you to preach for us, or perhaps learn you to be a jolly fellow like one of us; or what do you think of being tied and left here for a wolf bate?"

Poor Henry, young as he was, comprehended into what hands he had fallen. His hair rose on his head as he heard them utter their horrid curses and say that they hoped it would kill the canting hypocrites, as they called Mr. and Mrs. Howe; and call upon God to destroy them soul and body if ever they allowed them to set eyes on their petted and spoiled favorite again.

Tuttell and Callender, for the latter was the accomplice of this abandoned villain in the commission of this diabolical deed, the better to mislead Mr. Howe, went through swamps and untrodden tracts of land, and in a couple of hours were beyond any knowledge which the child had of the country. When they had advanced so far and crossed their track so often that they judged they had baffled all attempts of immediate pursuit, they began to remit the paces of their horses a little, and well it was for poor Henry. He was rather delicately made, and had never been used to the slightest fatigue. Besides, he was entirely unprovided with the means of riding comfortably in the present case, and every bone in him ached with a violence of pain that he never before felt. Then the storm came on. I have described, some pages back, the situation of this unfortunate little boy during the first part of the storm.

My reader has the knowledge of the situation of both father and child at this time. Could this knowledge have been imparted to the seeking and disconsolate parent, what anguish it would have spared him. How many sleepless nights and comfortless days

it would have saved him. The want of
this knowledge was the bitterness of the bitter portion of his existence. And yet it was
no doubt withheld for good and wise purposes.

When he awoke from the disturbed slumber which had weighed down his heavy
eyelids, the rain still poured and the wind
blew. His wet clothes chilled his limbs,
and the contrast between his present suffering and former comfort, again brought
the bitter tears. As they flowed, he felt, as
every one has at some time in his life, as
though his heart was bursting and all would
soon be over with him. This poor child in
his extreme distress, remembered the prayer
which he used to repeat as he knelt at his
mother's knee before he went to his comfortable bed, and when he arose from it; and
the recollection soothed him, although the
warm tears trickled faster down his cheeks
as these affecting recollections rushed full
upon his mind.

What a blessed thing it is, my dear young
friends, amidst all the changes and chances
of this vale of mortality and tears, to have

a Friend that no one can separate us from—
a Friend who goes with us wherever we
go; who remains with us wherever we remain; who is above us and around us, by
land and by sea, in sickness, in sorrow, in
death; who watches over our mortal body
when it is consigned to its clay-cold bed;
who will not suffer a hair of our head to
perish in the grave; but will raise these vile
bodies incorruptible and immortal! What
an unspeakable privilege, to love, fear and
trust such a friend!

The forlorn Henry felt this comfort to a
certain degree. He felt that this was the
only friend now left to him. They cannot
take away my Heavenly Father, he said;
and he repeated over to himself every one
of his prayers that he could recollect, and
then the little hymns which his mother had
taught him. These holy exercises soothed
and calmed his young heart. Callender and
Tuttell meanwhile said to each other, if
they intended to take the deepest revenge by
allowing the young talkative to live and not
to have him die, they must stop somewhere
and find a shelter from the storm; and on

his account as well as their own, endeavor
to obtain something to eat.

It was not long before they came to a
deep cypress swamp. The trees were all
hung around with festoons of long moss,
black and dismal to the eye, seeming at a
little distance like slips of black crape inter-
woven among the branches and leaves of
the trees. They entered this swamp, and as
they rode on, the horses stumbled among
hassocks and mud holes and cypress knees.
The thick covering of clouds that overspread
the sky and made the day like twilight,
deepened the gloom that always rests upon
these dense swamp forests. The lightning
gleamed upon the standing water and
showed its green and unwholesome appearance as it spread around on every side.
The two men made their way along, un-
heeding the danger of being thrown from
their horses and having their necks broken
on the cypress knees, and undismayed by
the desolation and forlornness of this immense grave above ground.

As the night began to shut in, Henry saw
a little in advance of them, a light that

seemed stationary. As they drew nearer
to it, he perceived that it came from a dwelling. It was a fire that burned brightly
and diffused around a cheerful light, which
brought a ray of comfort to Henry's heart
as it reminded him of the evening fire in his
father's house. They had left the swamp
a half a mile behind them by this time and
were close to the habitation. It was a log
cabin, rather larger than common, surrounded by a small clearing which was
bordered by thick woods on every side.

Well did Henry remember that a half a
dozen large dogs kept watch around his
father's door; and by a bark that might almost seem one of welcome, announced
friendly strangers. But here in this dark
place, on the verge of a dismal swamp,
every thing seemed governed by suspicion.
No dog barked. No sounds of any domestic animals were heard. Two or three bad
looking men with lowering countenances,
brought torch lights to the door in one hand,
and held a rifle in the other, while they
were surveying the strangers. Tuttell
spoke to them and with one of his peculiar

6

curses asked them if they did not know him. The answer was in the same kind of language; and forthwith there came out several negroes.

Callender and Tuttell dismounted, leaving their horses to the care of the negroes and entered the cabin. It was filled with men, women, children and negroes, in mingled confusion.

Henry would have been greatly relieved to have gone from the dark night and rain into a warm room, had there been a single thing in this dreadful place to cheer his sight or inspire him with the least degree of confidence in any one. But they were all wild and fierce looking people, and their very first words filled his mind with horror. He observed the two ruffians who had brought him off, to talk a moment with the man who appeared to be the chief person present, and then a low conversation passed among all the white people, accompanied by looks directed to him, from which he conjectured that he was the subject of all this conversation. They then pointed him to a dark corner beside a sick black boy, where

he was told to sit down; and no more notice
was taken of him for some time.

It would give little information to my
reader if I were to describe this place in de-
tail. It was an island in the centre of a
cypress swamp. The people were members
of the great chain of negro-stealers. The
women were thieves, and, in every way, of
abandoned character, and the men were fit
companions for them, practising every kind
of crime without control or remorse. Their
visible business, in case any honest person
passed that way, which hardly ever happened, was making shingles and articles of
that sort, or lumberers, as they were called.
Not far distant was a boatable water course,
down which their lumber might be trans-
ported to the Washita. But their real pursuit was to shelter and exchange stolen
goods and stolen negroes. People had been
known to disappear as they journeyed in
that vicinity with money about them.
There is no doubt but they would have
shed blood on any occasion for a very small
temptation; for they appeared to have no
compassion for any one, and they had learn-

ed to have no fear of God before their eyes. There is all reason to believe, that they would have perpetrated any crime without remorse or scruple, that would conduce to their interest or gratification.

The white people in this establishment were fourteen or fifteen in number, and there appeared to be nearly the same number of negroes. A smoking supper was soon on the table. When that was over, cards were brought forward. Whiskey was passed from one to the other, and curses deep and loud were continually on the lips of these miscreants as they celebrated their infernal orgies. Silver dollars and bank notes were staked upon the success of the games, and these very people who united to despoil others, were always quarrelling with one another because each one wished to cheat the other. Meanwhile poor Henry was assigned in company with the little negroes, a bone, a potato, and a piece of corn bread. Different as this fare was from what he had been accustomed to, he ate it eagerly, for he was very hungry. When sleep came over him, he laid himself down upon the hard floor, without pillow or covering, on the same spot where he had eaten his supper.

In the morning he fed in the same way as in the evening. Soon after the sun had risen, Callender and Tuttell were prepared to resume their journey. As Tuttell had carried Henry the greater portion of the day before, he insisted that Callender should take him as much of the day to come. Callender refused with threats and curses, alleging, that it was a foolish business the whole of it; that he had no grudge against Howe, and that they must have had less brains than a sucking pig, to use his phrase, when they took so much pains to vex a silly Methodist who lived quietly at Mount Prairie when people would let him; and he added again, that for his part he was determined to have nothing to do with carrying the brat. To this Tuttell replied that he supposed he would do as he pleased; that he had, however, promised to aid in the business and to carry it through; and that he ought to have found out that it was such a foolish business before he had enlisted in it. At any rate, he told him if he

6*

did not take his share in the affair and trouble, and he uttered a terrible oath as he said it, he would carry the boy a little way into the swamp and dash his brains out against a tree. He seemed to be fully bent upon his horrid purpose; and we may readily believe that a person who had so little reason to hate the father of this boy and yet would take so much pains to carry off the son merely to torment that father, would, when the occasion called for it, kill him.

Callender appeared to have the greatest touch of mercy and of human nature about him; for when there seemed no other way to save him from the merciless hands of Tuttell, he consented to take the poor boy up behind him. Just as the little fellow was put on horseback, one of the women too, showed that she had not altogether the heart of a tigress; for she went and took up an old wool hat and put it on his head, and then gave him a biscuit to eat on the way. As the child, affected with the first relenting that he had seen on this sad journey, dashed away the tears from his eyes, the woman actually reached forward and kissed him.

Away they rode again with the poor forlorn boy, through swamps and forests, he could form no kind of thought where; but it was towards the south-west. The next night he was obliged to sleep in the wild woods. The wretches covered themselves with blankets and laid down, telling him to take a log for a pillow, the grass for a bed, and the heavens for a covering, and to help himself. The little fellow shivered with the cold and the dew; but covered himself as well as he could with the autumnal leaves, said, Our Father who art in heaven, and prayed God to bless his dear father and mother, and brother and sister; and then the thought rose in his heart and sprung to his lips, that he would ask his heavenly Father to take him from the hands of these men to his house above. He then laid still, and Callender and Tuttell believed him asleep. They began to talk with each other about the folly of burdening themselves with the care of a poor brat of a boy. The one upbraided the other as the author of this folly.

They then threatened and cursed each other; and from that, began to talk about disposing of him. Callender was for carrying him back to some place where they might send him home. He said that he had no objection to do any sharp deed that was necessary—but that it burdened his conscience to commit a silly act of cruelty without motive or object. Tuttell said with a most dreadful oath that he had sworn with a curse upon his soul, that he would carry through the business as he had begun it. He allowed that the boy was a trouble, and proposed to put the business to a finish by killing him on the spot as he slept; and he even uttered a horrid jest on the mercy of sending the little hypocrite to heaven while he was asleep. Upon his saying this, Callender sprang up and declared in the most passionate terms, that he was afraid to go to sleep with such an infernal villain; one who would perpetrate such a horrid murder without object; and that before he killed the boy, he would have to kill him. Tuttell finding him resolute, softened and tried to coax his companion into confidence again. He succeeded in his attempt, and now that they were both in the same temper, it was

agreed that they should carry him on to a
certain place, which they named, on the Sabine. Tuttell went to sleep as he proposed
to black the boy, frizzle his hair, and sell
him for a negro. Callender answered that
this was a more thriving and Christian-like
project, and that he should not object to it.

All was then still, but the hooting of the
owls and the howling of the wolves. The
poor boy slept and dreamed that he was
sick, and that his mother came to give him
medicine. When he awoke, the stars glis-
tened through the trees. The cold damp of
the night wet his fair locks. The wretches
lay in deep sleep. But there is one eye that
never sleeps. Doubt not that this forlorn
child was under the immediate inspection of
the Father of the orphan, and he tempers
the wind to the shorn lamb. He preserves
the young of animals in the cold and in the
storms. In the extreme bitterness of a Ca-
nadian winter I have seen a little bird with
a body not larger than an acorn, hopping
and chirping amidst the snows, when man
was clad in furs or seated by a warm fire
in a tight room. Who warms the little

sprightly thing? The same Being that sustained this forlorn child, who had been nursed with the most watchful tenderness until this hard trial had come upon him.

One night, for purposes that he could not divine, they left him entirely alone just on the edge of a pine forest all the long night. His young heart shrunk within him as he heard the wolves howl. But He who giveth the beasts of prey their food, caused that they came not nigh him. He said his prayers and shed many tears, and finally wept himself to sound and dreamless sleep. When he awoke, the sun was in the sky and his tormentors had returned. They joked him and questioned him whether he had had a good meeting of it, using the term which the Methodists adopt when they break up a religious exercise.

They were seven or eight days wandering in the woods after this sort, before they arrived at the Sabine. They stopped now and then at houses full of wicked people such as I have described, blasphemers, gamblers and negro-stealers, persons, who for a price would murder any one. Little

Henry was always treated in one way. A bone, a piece of corn bread and a place with the little negroes, were invariably assigned him. One night they spent in a deep cavern full of these people. They caroused high, and gambled, and drank, and shouted, and fought through the night, and until the morning light shone full abroad. There was much in this dreadful place that I would describe, did I not fear that it would make my narrative seem like the stories told in books of fiction.

When they arrived at the Sabine, Henry found a settlement composed almost entirely of this sort of people. He was handed about from one family and one dark place, and one set of blasphemers, to another—sometimes treated with more and sometimes with less neglect. Sometimes he was hungry—sometimes when the child in him prevailed over his purpose not to cry, he wept, and then he was beaten and thrown to the ground. In the meantime, from being bitten by musquitoes and vermin, his body was covered with sores. His clothes were torn to rags; and had he not been a boy of

uncommon smartness and spirit, he would
have been as completely subdued and broken down in mind as he was forlorn in
body. But he had been taught to trust in
his heavenly Father. He had a sustaining
confidence that always existed in his young
heart, that in some way he should be sup-
ported through all his trial and finally be
brought to see his parents again.

But while his tormentors were carrying
on their various plans of vengeance, negro-
stealing, gambling and crime, they found
that for some former suspected misdeeds a
warrant was out to apprehend them on a
charge of murder. They both absconded in
the night, and the next morning Henry
awoke and arose from his customary place
of rest on the naked floor without any one
to claim him. Horrible as were the faces of
his tormentors to him, he had imbibed in
two months' endurance of their cruelties, a
kind of impression that they had a right to
exact his obedience; and strange as it may
seem, an added feeling of desolation came
over him as the people inquired where he
came from and what kind of people his pa-

rents were. They heard his sad story without apparent interest; but by adding what
he was able to relate to them concerning his
father and the circumstances of his having
been stolen away, to what they had heard
from Tuttell and Callender, they were led
to infer pretty nearly the true state of the
case. They told the child that they would
determine in two or three days what to do
with him.

Truth is, they partly entered into the malignant feelings of those who had practised
this revenge upon the father of the child,
and they were partly afraid, as they well
knew that they themselves were under suspicion of a great variety of crimes; that they
should be indicted as abettors of the crime
of child-stealing, and they were in a study
how to dispose of the boy. They did not
wish to have the burden of him themselves,
as he would be some expense and no profit.

While they were thus in doubt, the poor
little fellow had been so much exposed to
the weather and hardship, that he sickened
from mere suffering. He became raving
with fever. His once fair and silken hair

7

hung in a matted mass around his neck. His body became emaciated and his hands as bird's claws.

But God who first touched the human heart with pity, raised up an unknown friend to the poor boy in one of the women, who saw, pitied, and did all she could for him in the way of nursing and medicine. It went to her heart, as one would think it would to the heart of any one, to hear him in his delirium call her to him and ask her to say prayers and thanksgivings with him that he had once more got home to his dear parents. Then he would put his arms around her neck and embrace her as his mother. She would listen as he talked to his father and little brother and sister in his meek and subdued voice, of all the cruelties and sufferings he had experienced, until tears fell from her eyes. Such was the general tenor of his wandering thoughts. At other times he screamed with terror and implored help to escape from his supposed present tormentors, with cries of distress that would have thrilled any heart that was not of stone.

I should be sorry to prolong this gloomy recital. The child finally recovered, but looked like a breathing skeleton, pale, yellow, ragged, neglected, and what was more pitiable still, what he had passed through during his sickness had taken from him entirely all remembrance of his father's family and of the events of his past life. He had even forgotten to pray to his heavenly Father. As soon as the child was able to walk and ride, the people where he staid, carried him to a point on the Red River, above Natchitoches. They then by a slight reward, induced a Frenchman who was going down the river in a periogue, to take him in and carry him on, until he should reach a place where he could leave him in a situation to be seen and taken up by some one.

Accordingly during some of the most disagreeable days in the latter part of the winter, the French pedlar, for his periogue was loaded with articles which he intended to dispose of to the people who lived on the banks of the river, paddled down the stream with this destitute sufferer, leaving him in the periogue when he went on shore to trade. The pedlar seemed not entirely destitute of heart, for he arranged him a tolerably comfortable couch with his buffalo robe, and sometimes talked good naturedly to him, which cheered the poor child, although he could talk no French and the pedlar knew no more English than would enable him to say, *courage my preet boy.* He fed him too, as well as his supplies would admit. He shared his coffee with him and whenever he obtained a piece of fresh venison or cat fish, he remembered the sick child and broiled some of the best for him.

When the pedlar reached the village of Alexandria, he landed his periogue, and leading the child he ascended the bank and directed his steps to a poor looking house that stood near the river. He knocked at the door and it was opened by a woman. The Frenchman summoned all his English to ask her if she would allow his *leet gorcan* to rest himself for half an hour in her house. The woman consented. The

French pedlar disappeared and has not been seen in that quarter since.

The woman engaged in household occupations, did not take any notice of the child after the first look, she being accustomed to see sickly children around her from among the lower classes of the white people. But after two or three hours had passed, instead of half an hour, without seeing the Frenchman, she began to think it strange, and turned to question the boy. He had not spoken, because no one had said any thing to him when he first came in, and being weak and fatigued by the walk up the bank and to the house, and being used to neglect, he had leaned his head against the wall and fallen asleep. She awakened him and asked to whom he belonged and where he came from? He was not able to give a satisfactory answer to these questions, and she left him to go and tell the story of his being left with her, to one of her neighbors. This neighbor was violent, cruel, hardhearted and every way a savage woman, who lived near the jail and was the wife of the jailor. After this woman had heard the

7*

story, she proposed to go herself and see the child, and try if she could not get more information from him than her neighbor had obtained.

They went together and Henry was again questioned. But he could tell nothing more than that he had been very sick, and then he came down the river with a man that he had never seen before. When they asked him if he had a father and mother, he told them that he did not know. All that he could say in addition to what he had already said, was, that the people at the house where he was sick, sent him to the river. The wife of the jailor then asked her neighbor what she meant to do with the child if no one came to claim him? Her reply was, that she could not provide for him, and that as he was unable to assist himself, she should be obliged to give him into the care of the parish. The jailor's wife told her that she would relate to her husband the whole affair, and that as his business brought him acquainted with such matters, he would be the best person to arrange the future care of the boy.

Accordingly, application was made to the authorities of the parish in behalf of the child. Upon the jailor's wife offering to take care of him for a small sum, he was transferred to her.

CHAPTER III.

"Though hand join in hand, the wicked shall not be un-punished."

I should be glad to follow Callender as well as Tuttell through their subsequent fortunes. I think that in so doing, I might aid in impressing my youthful readers with the belief that in every case honesty, and goodness, and truth are the best policy; that in some way, either by an evil conscience, or sickness, or misery of some sort, or punishment by the hands of justice, or by all these together,—the wicked never fail to suffer for their guilt, even in this life. It is an important moral of which we ought never for a moment to lose sight, that crime and punishment are linked together by the hand of the Almighty—that his strength has forged every link of the chain, and that no man can break one of them. Let us never cease to remember the truth that this binding of misery to doing wrong and departure in any way from what is right, is as much a positive act of the Almighty, as it will be hereafter to punish the wicked in perdition.

But I am not informed as to what became of Callender. There is no doubt, however, that if he goes on in the commission of crime, even handed justice will sooner or later discover him. I am aware too, that my readers will feel less indignation towards him than Tuttell; because it is evident that unfeeling and brutal as he seemed to be, he was the instrument in the hand of providence in saving the child's life. Callender was in appearance careless, slovenly and brutish. There was nothing about him different from any common, large, stiff-jointed clown. Tuttell on the contrary, was a man of rather a fine appearance, with a bright complexion, blue eyes and fair hair, the last person, as a casual observer would suppose, to engage in such an atrocious project as that I have been relating, which could have originated only in the blackest and deepest malignity. He had something of the air and manner of a gentleman; and he had received a showy education, the principal point of which was the capability of writing a beautiful hand.

But observe the necessary consequence of carrying a guilty conscience. In making his way from the remote and untrodden forests of the Sabine towards the rising sun, he was obliged to wind along through swamps and bayous, like a revengeful Indian who is lurking to destroy some one whom he hates. He stopped here and there, at the same kind of places as those of which I have spoken before. Even there he devoured his food in guilty trembling, and as he stole onward in his hidden path, the very rustling of the leaves carried terror to his wicked heart.

At length he reached a part of the state of Mississippi, so remote from the chief scene of his villainies that he felt tolerably secure. This man was young in years, but he had become old in wickedness, while he was yet beyond the seas. When he came to this country, he plunged still deeper into crime, for he thought that in our wide country, especially in that part which he had late-

ly traversed, where there were such vast ex-
tents of forest, and swamp, and prairie unvis-
ited and almost unknown, offering so many
facilities for concealment and lessening so
much the chances of detection, he could outrage humanity and the laws with impunity.
The position too, on the frontier, gave him
great scope for the commission of crime.
But he had found that even there the ways
of transgressors were hard. He was often
obliged to fly from actual danger, and still
oftener from the imaginary terrors of an evil
conscience. He found that even where no
one could charge him with an actual crime,
there was always a certain kind of dark
suspicion attached to him; that no honest
man had confidence in him; that no decent
man would associate with him; that if in
the gatherings of young people, to which he
was allowed admittance, he addressed a
young woman of respectability, she shrunk
from him as though he was a suspected and
guilty thing. Besides, he said to himself,
as he felt all these things and reviewed his
past life, that one half the pains and industry which he had taken to make himself a

villain, would, if properly employed, have made him an honest man, and brought him property and consideration.

When he had arrived, therefore, as I have said, in Mississippi, he took a solemn resolution,—mark, my youthful reader,—that he would set himself resolutely to reform his outward conduct. He did not reproach himself for his want of religion, and good principles, and honesty, and mercy, and conscience. He foolishly thought that all within might remain, as it had been, and that he could be outwardly an honest man, and inwardly the same villain as before. But observe, that a bow that is bent always strives to unbend. A man that is acting a part is always under constraint, and it is next to impossible to sustain it any length of time without allowing something of the real character to show forth. Therefore the proverb says, that honesty is the best policy, the only policy, in fact, that can carry a man through. For be a man ever so crafty and cautious, by and by his real character will show itself through some unguarded part of his conduct.

But to return. Tuttell resolved to show himself an honest man, and to go into the employment of honest men. So he bought him an English grammar, a spelling book, an arithmetic and dictionary; and then put himself to the task of learning the duties of a master of a common English school. Being, as I have said, a tolerable scholar, writing a good hand, and gifted with a quick apprehension, he soon acquired a knowledge of the necessary routine of practice for his proposed profession. This done, he advertised for a school, produced testimonials from people in good standing, both in the old world and the Atlantic states, which he had forged. A place soon offered. for which he proposed himself, as a man who had just arrived in this country.

He was examined, went through his examination well, and was engaged as a teacher in a respectable school, with a handsome salary; and, had he been of good and firm principles, with a clear conscience, he might have been useful, respectable, respected, and happy, in one of the most important and useful occupations in society. For

8

the first few weeks he was very popular.
He began to feel the difference between the
life he had led and was now leading, and
rightly to estimate the feeling of standing
well, and moving among the decent and respectable in society. So much the more, as
he felt the value of his present good name
and standing,—so much the more terror he
felt at the thought of being detected in the
courses which he had led during the past.
The very extent of his fears and forebod-
ings, and management to prevent its being
known who and what he had been, finally
led to his ruin. The people around him, although they thought well of him, were occasionally struck with something in his manner and habits that they could not account
for. At times he had a look of absence, and
betrayed feelings that must spring from bitter remembrances. It was noted first by
one, and then by another, until it was a
matter of general surprise, that in all his
copies, and in all his writing in the school,—
and all scholars know how much masters
have to write,—he was never known to
write his full name in fine hand; but al-

ways used his initials.   Whenever a stranger inquired his name, he started, and answered with hesitancy.

As these facts fell under the observation
of different individuals, they fastened upon
their minds, and produced a conviction,
without their having been conscious, perhaps, of bestowing a thought on the subject,
that there was some mystery connected
with this man.

Much as he was changed externally in
condition and standing, some of his former
coadjutors in iniquity found him out; or at
least heard where and how he was situated.
They at first made merry with the idea that
the veteran villain, Tuttell, should be trans-
formed into a mere drudge of a school-master.   They laughed at him indeed with
their lips; but in the black depths of their
hearts they cursed him for deserting them
and going over to the enemy. They determined upon revenge.   Their first mani-
festation of this feeling was in writing an
anonymous letter to him, informing him
that they knew all about his present position,
and that although they despised his coward-

ly hypocrisy, if he would deposit a certain sum of money in a certain place for their use, they would allow him to sneak to the grave undiscovered, as a petty school-master.

My reader may judge how this unhappy man quailed and trembled as he read this letter. But something was to be done. The whole savings of three months' school-keeping were enclosed in a letter and left at the designated place. He knew but too well that the writer of the anonymous letter was acquainted with all that he had been as well as what he now was, and was both able and disposed to impart this knowledge to others.

But this first compliance only made way for more requests, which thickened upon him to such a degree that had he had twenty times his present means they would have consumed all. In order however to satisfy these greedy demands as far as possible, and at the same time make his peace with the father of the lost child and through him with society, he put a letter in the Natchez post office directed to Mr. Howe.

This letter reached its place of destination

and was given into the hands of Mrs. Howe
as her husband was absent. She opened it
with a trembling hand and a beating heart;
for although she had followed bones supposed to be those of her son to the grave,
and although she wore a lock of the fair
hair that was found in her bosom and for
months had mourned her lost son as dead,
in her constant meditation upon this dreadful visitation the thought had sometimes
arisen that perhaps he was yet alive. This
thought returned again and again, until her
mind became almost as excited as it had
been before they received the last sad information. It was not impossible. They
knew nothing with certainty, she said to
herself, and God might yet grant that she
should see her lost child in the flesh. In
this state of feeling, hope only slumbered in
her breast, ready to spring up afresh with
the slightest awakening. If a letter came
to the house or a stranger entered the door,
she instantly thought of the possibility that
she might hear of her son. As her eyes
glanced eagerly over the contents of this letter, the blood rushed into her veins, as

8*

though by a powerful revulsion of feeling every drop had been driven from her heart. Then it as suddenly and rapidly returned, and her face became pale again. Her strength failed her and she sank upon the floor. A domestic hearing her fall, ran in, sprinkled water upon her face and recovered her. As soon as she could sit up, she called all her faithful and attached servants around her and read the letter to them. The information it bore, was as follows.

"If Mr. Howe will enclose fifty dollars in a letter to the writer, at Natchez, and send the mother of the lost child, unaccompanied by any other person to a certain house in Arkansas," [which was clearly pointed out and so designated that there was no danger of mistaking it,] "with two hundred dollars more, she shall receive her child from the hands of a woman, to whom she must pay the two hundred dollars." It was written handsomely, and signed, "THOMAS TUTTY."

Her distracting impatience to be upon the spot where she could alone satisfy herself as to the truth of what the letter said, would hardly allow her to finish reading it before she requested Cæsar to saddle a horse for her and himself, that she might begin her journey. She could not think of leaving her children behind for a moment. Cæsar carried the little girl, and the little boy rode with her. The good blacks had busied themselves so effectually in the few moments that were given to preparation, that the travellers were fitted out comfortably.

After a few parting words of charge and kindness from Mrs. Howe to her household, they set off for Natchez. She was induced to go there by the wish to see the person who wrote the letter. She felt as though she should know all from him when she should see him. Her route lay through Monroe, the seat of justice for the parish of Washita. Her husband had many friends in that place, and one in particular to whom she could look for advice and assistance. But she was three hundred miles distant from this friend, and almost the whole of the long way was through a very thinly settled country, where she could ex-

pect nothing more than to find a cabin to
sleep in at night.

She well knew that it was a tedious, comfortless and lonely journey; but she did not
falter in her purpose and her courage was
not shaken. Maternal affection gave her
strength of body and mind, decision and
firmness, endurance and hardihood, and
overpowered every selfish thought. It was
in the month of January. In the climate of
which I speak, it has many beautiful days.
There is just coldness enough abroad in the
air to make the cheek glow, and yet feel
cold to the touch. The blood is stirred and
every living thing feels its life. But the day
on which the little party set forth to seek
the beloved and lost one was gloomy. The
wind made a sad sound as it passed over
the trees and disturbed the few remaining
sear leaves that were scattered among their
branches. They had not been on their way
two hours, before the little girl cried with
fatigue. The boy, calling all the man in
him to his aid, held out some time longer;
but he too, was finally overcome, and began to weep bitterly.

Fortunately they were near a cabin.
They stopped, rested and fed the little ones
and themselves, and then resumed their
route. At night they came to one of the
comfortable rustic dwellings that are sometimes met with in this back country. Every
thing around bore the impress of homely
comfort and abundance. The double cabin
stood in the midst of the plantation, and a
little in advance of the out-houses and negro quarters. Even these had a look of
snugness, as though the indwellers were sober, orderly and happy. A fine corn and
wheat field and a potato patch, the larger
part of which, from its parallel lines of little
round hills of equal height and size, was
marked as the dominion of that important
article in southern living, the sweet potato.
When these little smooth hills are completely overrun with the handsome vine, bearing
a thick covering of delicately shaped leaves
of a most beautiful deep green, which be-
longs to this vegetable, they offer a charming sight. These fields and a garden spread
around the clusters of cabins—a large peach
orchard neatly enclosed with a picquet

fence, grew on a line but a little distant from the double cabin, which was inhabited by the master and his family. In front of this was a large turfed yard, on which had been left standing a few of the noble forest trees. Here in the cool shade the children played in summer, and here in the mild warmth of the Spring and Autumnal sun, they built their little houses, fenced and planted their gardens of a foot square, and acted out all the simple thoughts of childhood. The remainder of the large tract of enclosed land was one extensive cotton field.

As Mrs. Howe approached the gate with her faithful servant and the tired little ones, her respectable appearance and the circumstances of her travelling alone with her children and servant, drew attention from the head of the establishment, who stood near. He opened the gate for her to enter, and in a few words she told him who she was. He had heard the story of her loss, and knew Mr. Howe from report. He welcomed her kindly and accompanied her into the house, where they found his wife. When she too heard the story, the woman and the

mother rose in her heart, and tears sprang
to her eyes. She seated Mrs. Howe by the
fire, uncloaked the little boy and girl, and
kissed them as she thought of the lost brother they were seeking. The cheerful fire
blazed high, and shed its light and warmth
upon the travellers, and displayed beds in
the two corners of the room, covered with
home-made counterpanes of snowy white-
ness, and looking as though tired limbs
must rest refreshingly upon them. When
supper was prepared, the family with their
guests seated themselves around a plain
table made of cypress, but spread with neat-
ness, and offering a bountiful and excellent
repast of food, to which the children were
accustomed.

Supper being ended, they gathered again
around the fire. The children cracked nuts
together—the parents talked much and
solemnly of the afflictions that come upon
all who live on the earth; and the heart of
the mourning mother was comforted by the
sympathetic and cheering tones with which
these friendly strangers discoursed upon her

great affliction, and told her to hope for the best.

The travellers awoke the next morning invigorated. The mother dressed her children, heard them say their prayers as they knelt before her with folded hands, adding of themselves the petition which she had taught them for their absent brother while he was supposed alive, and then opening the door, they looked abroad. The sun was just rising, and the sky gave the promise of a bright day. The cows were standing ready to be milked, and in their way claiming admittance to their calves. Oxen with their ruminating looks champed corn in one spot. In another, a dozen horses, some looking, as they arched their proud necks and exhibited their graceful movements, as though they felt themselves the noblest animals in existence—others formed swift of foot, seeming, as they sprang away, curveted and returned, the embodied images of fleetness; and then the more still and worn ones, whose appearance marked them, as the useful assistants of man in his labors, were receiving their portion of food. The mingled sounds of life that arose from all these animals, the barking of the dogs, the bleating of sheep, the cackling and crowing of fowls, and the happy voices of the negroes as they prepared for the employment of the day, came upon the fresh and spirit-stirring air, as the glad awakening of so many living things to the light and glory of the unclouded sun.

Breakfast again assembled all the inmates of "this rude dwelling in the solitude," around one table. They ate in thankfulness, and arose to separate and perform their different duties. Followed by kind wishes, Mrs. Howe and her little party set forth on their journey. The boy and girl talked cheerfully to their mother and each other as they rode along. The current of a child's feeling is easily changed. They were fresh and untired, and delighted with every thing. As their mother listened to them, she was beguiled of her sad thoughts. The sun now rode high, and his light and warmth penetrated the depths of the forest. The birds came from their nests to sing their glad song, and the woods seemed almost alive with their notes. The children never tired in admiring the red birds as they flew across the path before them, looking like a gleam of crimson light. This day's journey was pleasant. The little boy and girl were becoming accustomed to the fatigue of travelling, and did not become fatigued and discouraged as before.

They were not so fortunate in a stopping place at night, as they had been the night before, but they did not complain. The next day their path lay through a swamp. This was very unpleasant for Mrs. Howe, who had not been much from home since her marriage, and knew very little of the difficulties of travelling. But she made light of it, and went through the water with a firm heart. All the faces that she saw were strange to her, but no one treated her with rudeness.

At the close of the eighth day, she reached Monroe. Her husband's friend was surprised to see her; but his reception of her was none the less cordial. She told him her business, and gave him the letter she had received from Natchez, and added, that she had come herself, because her husband was absent on a long journey. In the evening, as they were seated in a quiet room, by the fire, he told her the plan which he thought she had better pursue. In the first place, he advised her to remain where she was until her husband returned. When he reached his own house, he would certainly be informed where she had gone, and of the circumstances that induced her to go. He would then come to her, and they could journey together to Natchez. Meanwhile this friend proposed that himself should write to Thomas Tutty, and enclose in the letter fifty dollars; and that he should accompany this letter by one to the postmaster at Natchez, containing an account of the loss of the child, and every thing known in connection with the event.

To this should be added a request, that the postmaster would find some means to keep under his eye the person who should inquire for the letter directed to Thomas Tutty, until he could be examined legally, and upon no condition to allow him to escape. Mrs. Howe consented to this plan.

The letters were written and sent.   Cæsar
returned to his master's house, and in three
days after he reached home his master arrived there also.   Mr. Howe was not visibly
so much agitated as his wife had been, by
the information which he now received.
But could his heart have been laid open, it
would have displayed the same depth of
parental affection, the same agony of suspense as he was thus again rendered uncer-
tain as to the fate of this cherished and almost idolized boy, and the same determination to sustain any endurance to satisfy
himself as to the truth or falsehood of the
new statement of the case.

He soon joined his wife at the house of
his friend.   Mrs. Howe received her husband with a burst of tears.   She had had
strength and self-dependence while no one
was near for her to lean upon.   Now, that
she was no longer called upon to act, the
power to do so seemed to pass from her.
They talked together of their renewed hopes
and fears, and endeavored to aid one another
in acquiring resignation, and moderation,

and firmness to meet the result of this new information, be it what it might.

They set off together for Natchez, leaving their children in safety under the care of their friend. When they reached Natchez, Mr. Howe repaired immediately to the post-master. He found that the post-master had detained in custody the man who inquired for the letter directed to Thomas Tutty. Accompanied by the postmaster, Mr. Howe went to see this person. It was Tuttell. He had himself asked at the post office for a letter, directed as I have mentioned. The postmaster made some delay in making change, as he paid the postage, and thus kept the man on the spot, until the officer, for whom he had sent when the inquiry was first made, arrived, and apprehended him. He was tried before a magistrate, up-on the information that had been furnished by Mr. Howe's friend at Monroe. He would confess nothing, but threw the whole burden of proof upon the magistrate, and was sulky, shrewd, and pertinaciously obstinate in his purpose. He would not admit the identity

9*

of the hand-writing with his own, and denied that Thomas Tutty was his name.

He affirmed that he knew where the child was, when he was charged with having fabricated a falsehood in the letter, which it was supposed he wrote, merely for the base purpose of extorting money from the affection of the parents; but defied them to prove that his name was Thomas Tutty, or that he wrote the letter in question.

He was, however, committed to prison, on the suspicious fact of having inquired for the letter. Now that Mr. Howe was on the spot, he was again tried. A deep interest was taken by many in this strange and terrible affair. Every effort of ingenuity was exhausted on this trial, in the endeavor to obtain something from the prisoner that might furnish a clue, by which it might be ascertained whether the child was alive; and if so, where he was to be found; but it was all to no purpose. Tuttell told the father, that in a certain place, where it was supposed he would pass in search of his child, he would find clothes which resembled those usually worn by the little Henry, and bones resembling those of a child of his years. But, he assured him that they were not the bones of his child, but of an animal, placed there to induce him to believe that his son was dead.

When Mr. Howe mentioned that one of his neighbors had led him to a certain spot, and showed him, as he then supposed, the bones of his lost child, Tuttell requested him to describe the spot. After hearing the description, he said that they had been moved; for that place was not the one where he had known them to be laid. Notwithstanding his avowal of this knowledge, and his hardihood in persisting that he knew where the child was, the parents were just as much in the dark, with regard to the actual fate of their child, as they had been at first. Nothing that the father, or mother, or lawyers, or magistrate said, or did, could extort from this man the slightest information beyond what I have already mentioned, imparted, as it would seem, to harrow up still more the feelings of the parents, and still keep them in a state of agonizing suspense.

In the course of the examination, it became

evident that the prisoner was perfectly conversant with all the swamps, and bayous, and passes, and bye-paths, and hiding places, that lay between Natchez and the settlement where Mr. Howe lived. He was questioned and cross questioned on this point by people who had traversed the country as surveyors, and knew every mile of it. His minute and accurate particularity in answering, surprised them; but they inferred from it, that as much knowledge in such a person could have been sought and acquired only for purposes of crime or concealment, it was most probable that he had not only committed the wicked act for which he was now arraigned, but many crimes in that country.

Tuttell was again remanded to prison. During the night following this examination, a number of the citizens of Natchez, stimulated by their intense interest, the warm blood of the south, and their impatient fondness for summary justice, went to the prison, took him out, and whipped him severely. Before they began, they told him what they intended to do, if he did not answer the questions they asked. They then demanded where the child was? He would not reply, and they commenced their chastisement. Still he said nothing. They ceased at intervals long enough to tell him, that, whenever he chose to impart the information, which he acknowledged himself to possess, they would desist.

Tuttell bore the infliction for some time, with the same sulky silence that he had hitherto maintained upon this point. But finally the point of endurance was passed, and he told the people to stop and he would tell all he knew about it. He then said, that if they would send to a certain house, between forty and fifty miles from Natchez, in Mississippi, they would there find people, who could tell them where the child was. The sheriff, who stated that he disapproved of the proceedings in regard to the chastisement, and was, moreover, ill at the time, was no sooner apprised of this information, than he started at midnight for the designated house.

When he reached the house, to which Tuttell led him, he discovered with the first look, that the people were respectable, and knew nothing of Tuttell, or the child, and that it was only a pretence of his to escape from the whipping. As they returned from this useless and fatiguing ride, the sheriff tried his individual powers at persuasion and representation upon Tuttell. He told him, that it would be much the wisest way for him to tell honestly all that he knew about this mysterious affair; and if he did not know where the child now was, to acknowledge his ignorance. He made a strong appeal to the feelings of humanity, which, as a man, a human being, he ought to possess. But it was of no use. Tuttell had become doggedly sullen and silent again.

On their arrival at Natchez, no new steps could be taken in the affair. All were convinced that Tuttell had been concerned in the stealing of the child; but that he no longer knew any thing of its present condition, and had been induced to what he had done, merely to obtain money, by sporting with parental affection and anxiety. The proper authorities consented to the enlargement of the prisoner, on what is called *nolle prossequi*, on condition that he should return with the parents, in the hope that promised rewards, or threats, or a returning sense of justice and humanity, when he should be on the spot, where he had brought this sorrow upon these good and affectionate parents, would yet induce him to put them on a clue to finding their son.

He was accordingly discharged from prison. and accompanied the parents across the Mississippi on their route towards home. It had been purposely intimated to him that unless he would frankly communicate to Mr. Howe, on the journey, all that he knew about the child, as soon as they should have travelled beyond the settlement, he would be put to death. After they had passed through Concordia, on the west bank of the Mississippi, and as they rode on through the heavily timbered land, half swamp, half bottom, which lies beyond, offering nothing to the eye but trees, whose naked and black branches looked still blacker through their partial envelope of long moss, and pools of stagnant water, along with bayous, equally unpleasant in appearance, Tuttell asked Mr. Howe what he intended to do with him. The reply was, if he persisted in withholding information about the child, he would be handed over to the civil authorities, to be dealt with for other criminal acts which had recently come to light. Mr. Howe wore pistols in his belt, for self-defence, during a journey with such a companion. Tuttell, upon receiving this reply, rushed upon Mr. Howe, seized one of his pistols, and snapped it at his breast. Although Mr. Howe had loaded and primed it himself, it fortunately missed fire. Thus disappointed in his purpose, of taking the life of this man, whom he had before so deeply injured, he darted forward to a bayou, which they were approaching, plunged in, probably intending to swim over it and escape, and was drowned.

The only visible hope of a clue to unravel this mysterious and tragical affair had now vanished. The parents, sick at the heart from such repeated and aggravated disappointments, felt as though hope on this point had forever expired within them. They had abundant time, as they retraced the long way home, to discuss the sad subject, and examine it in every point of view. In reviewing Tuttell's conduct, it was difficult to reconcile the assertion which he always obstinately persisted in making, that he knew where the child was, with his determination not to avow his knowledge any farther than he pleased, which he equally resolutely maintained.

His purpose could be influenced and altered, and his obstinacy conquered upon other points; but upon this he was immovable, and unchangeable. As I have said, the general conclusion was, that he really did not know where the child was. But it would seem that the natural course for a person who, like Tuttell, never had a feeling that was not prompted and governed by interest, that is, by what he thought was for his interest, would have been, when he found that he could not gain in the way of reward or safety, by obstinacy and silence, to confess his ignorance, and throw himself upon the mercy of the father, who was known to be a humane man and a Christian.

10

A thousand conjectures have been made as to the motives which had induced this unhappy man to pursue a course so opposite to the common order of things in human nature. It ended, as we have seen, in his ruin and death. The most probable view of the case is, that when he found that instead of dealing with the father, he had to undergo a legal trial, and be confined in prison, the dogged sullenness and obstinacy of his nature rose strong within him, and that he followed its impulse, even when he knew that it would lead him to inevitable ruin.

While Tuttell was in prison at Natchez, he had requested that a trunk, containing his clothing, might be brought from the settlement, where he had been keeping school. When preparation was made for his accompanying Mr. Howe to his home, this clothing was transferred into portmanteaus. Mr. Howe now examined the portmanteaus to see if they contained any papers. He found a package of letters wrapped in a thick envelope, that did not seem to have been opened for some time. They were not superscribed with the name Tuttell. They

were written from a father to his son, who,
it appeared, had just set up in a small business in Dublin, in Ireland, and were dated
from a town in the interior.

From the letters, the father would have
been said to belong to the middling class,
and to have had a small property. Frequent mention was made in them of the
young man's mother, his brother, and two
sisters. They were not very well written,
and indifferently spelt; but abounded with
manifestations of parental affection, and ex-
pressions of anxiety and fear that the young
person to whom they were written, would
be drawn into bad company and habits, and
be led to forget the sober and religious ways
in which he had been reared at home. Al-
lusions were made to former errors which
the young man had committed; not in a re-
proachful manner, but that they might
serve as warnings for the future.

To be brief, Mr. Howe gathered from
reading them, that Tuttell was the son to
whom they were addressed, and that Tuttell had begun life with fair prospects, a
good constitution, a good mind, a good per-

son, and in easy circumstances for a young
man.   But these blessings had been all
thrown away upon a character spoiled by
indulgence and the want of proper correc-
tion and restraint.   A sketch of the conduct
of this man from childhood to the point of
his self-inflicted death, will serve, with slight
variations, for the story of thousands who
have gone down to destruction in the same
way.   Nature gave him strong passions and
good capacities.   He was allowed to foster
these passions in the very germ.   When he
displayed temper towards his father and
mother, or brother and sisters and little
playmates, it was not properly checked.
He was not early taught the necessity of being just in all his actions.   Improper requests which he made, were granted; and
when he was refused at first, the refusal
was not persisted in; thus leaving an impression in the mind of the child, that there
was no real reason why he should have
been denied what he wished at all, and
that it was done from caprice alone.

From these causes, the boy imperceptibly
derived the conviction that there was no

such thing as right and wrong, and that if he gained his point, no matter how, it was all that was worth considering. He now began, whenever he thought it would be for his advantage, to tell falsehoods. For the first faults of this character that were discovered, he was chidden, perhaps, but he was not told strongly, what a disgraced and abhorred thing a liar is. He was not told that liars in their hearts despise themselves —that honest men shun them, and that God will cast them from him. The miserable parents, it may be, were so weak and guilty, that they concealed, instead of punishing the wickedness, through pride, lest others should know that one of their children had told a lie. He was mischievous at school; and the parents, instead of aiding his masters to cure his evil propensities by proper discipline, became angry with them, and removed him first from one school and then from another. He was finally expelled from a respectable one, under circumstances of disgrace. His parents took him home, and when he had reached the proper age, they set him up in business. At first, he

10*

selected for his city acquaintances idle young men, who, if they were not positively wicked, were ready to become so. Such society constantly operated to weaken any good impressions that had clung to him, and to strengthen all the bad ones that had gathered around his heart and mind. He soon took the next step in the downward road. From indolent and reckless associates he proceeded to those who had made the first advances in crime, and with them he was dissipated.

He now went on sinning more and more, until for some violation of the laws, he was in danger of public punishment. To avoid this, he fled from his country and came to America. After he arrived here, he endeavored to obtain money in dishonest ways. He was suspected, and he hastened to leave a spot where honest men understood him, and coldly past him by, and to hide himself in regions that seemed almost beyond the reach of law. He descended the Mississippi, ascended the Red River, and on the frontier of that portion of our country, he found the band of thieves, negro stealers

and murderers of which I have spoken. He
joined himself to them and became one of
the most active members. When his guilty
career closed in death, no one mourned for
him, and no one remembered him, except to
detest his conduct.

CHAPTER IV.

" For this my son was dead, and is alive again ; was lost, and is found."

A brief account of the events which I have here detailed, was published in the first number of " The Western Quarterly Review " for 1827. ˙ It excited much interest. What person that had a heart could read the simple and unadorned facts, recorded in the story of the lost child, without feeling sympathy for the parents and pity for the child. The incidents of the story awaken and excite the better feelings of our nature. In the section of Louisiana, near the places where the event occurred, after it was generally known, as parents sat together and talked of it, they would take their children into their arms and determine in their hearts to be more strict in the discharge of their duties towards them, while they were yet spared to them. Thus the story was not without its good results.

The Editor of the Western Quarterly Review received letters from different portions of the country, containing accounts of children, singularly situated, and apparently taken away from parents or friends, of whom they had lost the remembrance. They had come into the vicinity of the writers, and each one taking a benevolent interest in the parents of the lost child, of whom they had read, hoped that the child whom he described might prove to be the lost son of Mr. Howe. But on investigation, circumstances were brought to light which satisfied the minds of those who looked into the matter, that neither of these children were Henry Howe.

The information, however, thus received, showed, that in our country there are many children who have in some way been separated from their parents, and live as orphans in the most unhappy sense of the term; orphans, who have living parents by whom they are mourned, as dead.

Mr. and Mrs. Howe reached Monroe on

their return, in safety, and found their children well. Their kind friend sympathised with them, as they related the entire failure of their last hope. In a few days they took leave of him, and proceeded on their journey homeward. They spent a night with the friendly people who entertained Mrs. Howe so kindly, the first night after she had left her own house on her way to Natchez. The next day they reached home. The harrowing scenes which they had passed through, since they left their own quiet and pleasant dwelling, had created for a time in their minds so strong an excitement, that when the cause of this state of feeling was suddenly removed, a natural repulsion of feeling reduced them to a state of quiet sadness, almost approaching to apathy. The spirit of repose that seemed to overshadow and pervade every thing around, was to them all that they wished.

The faithful servants were delighted to see them: but with a tact inspired by affection, they refrained from making any inquiries about "poor little master Henry," as they looked upon the dejected faces of their

master and mistress. As the husband and
wife again resumed their ordinary employ-
ments, and busied themselves in the per-
formance of their usual duties, they succeeded in a degree in their wish to divert their
thoughts from the sad subject which had so
long engrossed every feeling.

In this manner two years and a half
passed over the heads of this family. They
were now again comparatively happy.
Time had blunted the keen edge of their
sorrow. Mrs. Howe, as her maternal heart
was gladdened by the growth in beauty and
knowledge of the happy and innocent dear
ones who remained to her, sometimes felt
as if the shade of gloom which occasionally
came over her mind in the midst of so many
blessings, was sinful. She endeavored always to seem soberly cheerful, and to await
calmly whatever of good or ill, Providence
might yet have in store for them.

Near the time of which I speak, among
the causes brought before the district court
of the Parish of Rapide, in Louisiana, then
in session, in Alexandria, on Red River, was
one against the wife of the jailor of that

place for mal-treating and abusing a child
in her keeping. The charges to be estab-
lished against the woman were in general
those of cruelty, in beating the child unmer-
cifully, and without any cause, and those in
relation to his not being furnished with
proper and necessary food and clothing.   In
the course of the trial, the boy was brought
into court. He seemed to have been the
heir of long suffering and humiliation ; being ragged, meagre, and apparently stinted
in his growth. The wounds and bruises
that he had received from the hands of those
through whose keeping he had passed, were
such that he will probably carry the marks
of them to his grave. The woman was
acquitted of the charges against her, in consequence of peculiar circumstances that excited their compassion. But strong feeling
was called forth in behalf of the child.   Notwithstanding his squalid appearance, produced by suffering of every sort, he seemed a
boy of uncommon quickness, and his countenance interested all who looked upon it
from the melancholy expression of his fine
eye.   In the course of the trial, as the jail-

or's wife related all that she knew of the child, and the manner in which he came into her hands, the thought occurred to several persons that this might be the lost child, whose story had spread far and wide and excited so much interest. But there was one difficulty in the way of this belief.

The age of the child now before the court did not seem to agree with what was supposed to be that of the lost child. It was known that his age must be between seven and eight years; whereas the boy under examination was judged to be only between five and six. This circumstance prevented any steps, that would otherwise have been taken, in the mother. The poor little fellow was, however, taken from this woman, and placed under the care of a family who lived on the bank of the river, opposite to Alexandria. He was here comfortably clothed, well fed, and kindly treated. About a month after the trial had taken place, Col. O., an intimate friend of Mr. Howe, arrived in Alexandria. As he was conversing with some gentlemen of his acquaintance, two or three days after his arrival, one of them in-

11

troduced the story of the late trial, and mentioned that some had thought for a short
time, that the lost child was this very boy.

Col. O. listened with intense interest to
the recital, and as soon as it was concluded,
although it was then nine o'clock in the
evening, he said that he would immediately
cross the river and see the child.   He had
spent some time in Mr. Howe's family before Henry was carried away, and he knew
him perfectly well.   He had amused himself by talking with him a thousand times.
He had aided the father in searching for
him.   From these circumstances, and from
the knowledge which Col. O. had of some
peculiar marks upon little Henry, he felt as
if no change that suffering and ill treatment
could bring upon him, would prevent his
recognizing him instantly.

Accompanied by several gentlemen, he
proceeded across the river.   He told the
family with whom the child now was, his
business, and asked to see him.   He was in
bed and asleep at that moment.   On being
awakened, and told that some gentlemen
wished to see him, he got up and went, as he

was directed, to them. Col. O. took up the candle, and held it so that the full light fell upon the child's face. The surprise of this unfortunate boy may be imagined, as he saw himself thus examined. But he said nothing; for he had learned the hard lesson already, which taught the necessity of his keeping his thoughts and feelings under control. Col. O. saw a likeness to Mr. Howe in his face, and his eye was unchanged; but the other features of the face were altered. Eagerly and trembling, from the strength of his awakened feelings, he proceeded to look for the marks of which I have spoken.

One was on the head of little Henry, and had been left by a large swelling, which suppurated, and was lanced. The hair never came thick upon the spot again. Another was upon a nail of one of his fingers, which had been bruised, and thus acquired an unchangeable black spot. A third was a large mole on his right shoulder. These were all found by Col. O. upon the child before him.

He now clasped the child in his arms, and tears fell fast upon his cheek. The gentlemen who had accompanied him, could not witness such a scene without being deeply affected, as they congratulated Col. O. upon the joyful discovery.

Henry had been surprised at first; but as the examination advanced, and when he at last felt himself clasped in the arms of Col. O., and his face wet with tears from the eyes of his father's friend, he was stupified with astonishment. Col. O. after thanking and satisfying the people of the house for the kindness with which he understood they had treated Henry, recrossed the river with him.

Any person of a humane heart can conceive the happiness of Col. O., as he laid his head upon his pillow for the night. The next morning, Henry accompanied him to a shop of ready-made clothing, and in a short time the little fellow was handsomely clad once more. When he came forth, looking so neat from head to foot, and his countenance brightened by the affection and attention which all around bestowed upon him, a person who had seen him in his days of humiliation, would not have recognized the

ragged, meagre, and disconsolate child, in the handsome and interesting boy, who walked by the side of Col. O.

This gentleman was obliged to go to New Orleans before he could carry Henry to Mount Prairie. A steamboat was to leave Alexandria for New Orleans the following day. In it Col. O. took passage for himself and his charge. Henry had seemed so passive and silent, since any thing had been known of him by the people of Alexandria, that it was thought his feelings had become deadened by his sufferings. Col. O. missed him during the day, and went in search of him. He found him weeping behind some trees that stood near the jail.

When he saw Col. O. he wiped his eyes and tried to check his sobs. This kind friend asked him what made him cry— with tears standing in his own eyes, he replied in an uninterrupted voice, that before he had any body to speak kindly to him, or do any thing for him, and while he lived with the jailor's wife, who used to beat him so much, he had been often sent to that spot to find a rod which this woman used in

11*

whipping him, until her unfeeling nature was satisfied with the degree of pain she inflicted. He then went on to say, that after she had finished, he used to steal off, and come here to lay down upon the ground and cry, and wish that he was dead; and that now he had felt as though he must see that place again, and that when he did see it he could not refrain from crying.

Col. O. was touched by this incident; but he rejoiced in it as affording proof that his sensibility was still keen and unblunted. The morrow came, and the steamboat moored off. Henry stood on the guards, and looked back on the receding bank where he had endured so much misery, and who can tell what were his thoughts and feelings, child though he was? The passengers on board had heard his story, and they all treated him with attention and kindness. He was pleased with this mode of travelling, and when they came upon the broad Mississippi and swept past the noble plantations on the coast, his eye kindled with delight.

As I have said, all recollection of the period of his life, which passed before he was

taken sick on the Sabine, had entirely vanished. He knew nothing of father or mother, sister or brother, or friend. He had
forgotten his own name. All the tenderness
and instinctive affection of filial feeling he
bestowed upon his new benefactor; and he
heard with surprise, not unmixed with apprehension, that he was to pass from his
care to that of a father.

The steamboat arrived safely in New Orleans. Col. O. left his charge with the cap-
tain of the boat, and walked into the city.
Almost the first acquaintance that he met
was Mr. Howe. He had come to New Orleans on business, and had but just arrived.
The greeting of the friends was cordial and
affectionate, and they walked on together.
After the common inquiries and replies that
take place on such occasions, Col. O. asked
Mr. Howe if he had heard any thing with
regard to his lost Henry since the death of
Tuttell. A momentary sadness came over
his countenance, as he replied, that he had
ceased to hope upon that point, and that his
whole aim now was to be contented, and to

resign himself to the belief that he should see his child no more.

Col. O. approved of his determination, and then added, that he knew how much his friend had suffered from having been left to indulge unfounded hopes and expectations by persons, who, perhaps, really thought that they had made a discovery in relation to the child. He went on to say, that he had lately met with a boy near the age of his lost son, who interested him much. The parentage of this child was not known; but he thought he could discover a likeness in his face to Mr. Howe. With strongly awakened feelings, Mr. Howe now questioned his friend in relation to the circumstances under which he had found the child, and whether he had any reason to believe him to be his son. Col. O. in reply, acknowledged that he had reason so to believe. Mr. Howe requested a direction to the place where the child was, and as soon as he received it, he turned to go towards the river, saying, that he would take the first boat to Alexandria. Col. O. walked on with him, and endeavored to calm the visi-

ble agitation of his friend, by representing
that it might be a mistake, and that he almost regretted thus to awaken hopes that
might prove as delusive as others had done.

Mr. Howe made an effort over himself,
and said that he would be calm. He did
seem so. They were now in sight of the
steamboats. Col. O. looked upon his friend
with a glad countenance, as he said, "I
have deceived you upon one point. The
little fellow came down with me, and we
shall find him in that boat," pointing, as he
spoke, to the one which brought him. Mr.
Howe turned pale, but he quickened his
steps. They entered the handsome cabin
together. Mr. Howe could go no farther
than the first chair. Henry, said Col. O. to
the child, as he stood looking towards the
streets of the city, "come to me; I have
brought a gentleman to see you." Henry
approached, and the moment his father's
eye rested upon his countenance, "My son,
my son!" said he, "it is indeed my son!"

His father clasped him to his breast, and
held him as though he feared he should
again lose him. His overcharged heart re-

lieved itself in tears that may not be called weak, for they spring from the purest movements of our nature. No change that four, or even five years could bring over the countenance of the child could prevent recognition from the heart and eye of the parent. But, as if to confirm himself beyond a doubt in his joy, Mr. Howe looked first at his son's head; then at his finger nail; and lastly, at the mole. The marks were all familiar to his eye, and he found them all there.

Henry trembled in his father's embrace like an aspen leaf; but he felt that here was nothing but kindness and love, and as he looked upon the face of his father, dim and indistinct remembrances arose in his young mind, awakened by the passing thought that he had somewhere seen it before. Mr. Howe was. as I have said, a religious man, and his first defined thought was thankfulness to God. "Oh God," said he, "now lettest thou thy servant depart in peace." "He was dead and is alive again. He was lost and is found."

I shall not attempt to portray this scene

any farther. There are certainly no hearts that cannot imagine it by looking in upon themselves. Mr. Howe and his friend hastened their business, and in a few days they were on board a magnificent steamboat, which plowed the mighty wave of the Mississippi, on its upward way, with power and a rapidity that seemed to distance every thing but the breeze. We can all fancy how the time passed between this long-severed father and son, and what was the character of the conversations they held together, as they thus journied towards home.

I need only observe, that Henry, once more within the action of parental tenderness, soon began to catch the filial impulse anew; and before they reached Mount Prairie, he felt what a blessing a father was, and that this blessing was once more his own.

It was still a hundred miles from the point on the Washita where they left the steamboat, to the habitation of Mr. Howe. They took horses at that point, and joyfully travelled through the woods and prairies towards home, in which their arrival would create such gladness and rejoicing. When the dear spot was once more in view, Col. O. went forward to prepare the mother for her happiness, as unexpected as it would be great. It was a beautiful spring evening. Their servants were coming from their work. The birds were whistling sweetly in the woods. The domestic fowls were uttering their cheerful noises, as the diminishing light of the day closed in. The dogs welcomed the returned master with their affectionate, though inarticulate demonstrations of attachment. But now Col. O. was seen coming from the house followed by Mrs. Howe and her children. I have not words to describe the scene, as this mother, in the unutterable fondness of a maternal heart, clasped the dear boy to her bosom and kissed him a hundred and a hundred times. The servants had heard the glad tidings, and they gathered around the group, impatient to see their long lost favorite, and hear how he had been found.

This was a family, as we have seen, in which every thing was resolved into the act and the will of the providence of God; and it was only in saying to this gracious and adorable being, "thy will be done," that they had sustained this dreadful visitation.

I leave my young readers to ·picture to themselves the prayers and thanksgivings with which this evening closed, and the renewed caresses bestowed upon Henry as his mother left him in his bed, to retire to her own. His younger brother and sister had put their little arms around his neck, and were lying on each side of him asleep.

The next morning was Sabbath. The good Methodist minister learned that the lost child had been found, early in the morning. The settlement assembled as usual, at the rustic hours of worship. The minister arose and gave as his text,—"My son was dead, and is alive again. He was lost, and is found." He spoke to parents of their obligation to bring up their children in the love and fear of God. He spoke of the highest earthly happiness, domestic affection and the being blessed with good children. He spoke of the satisfaction which parents have in seeing their children in health and happiness around the paternal hearth. On this

12

occasion, he gave his sermon a practical application to the case I have recorded. He spoke of the mercy of God in having sustained the lost child through so much affliction and misery, and having brought him back to the arms of his parents. He said, that the affection of Jehovah for sinners wandering from him, and their own mercies, was of the same nature, but far stronger in degree, with that which these parents felt for their returned child. His closing words were—" Yes, a thousand times more joy than these parents feel to embrace once more this their son, who was dead, and is alive again, who is lost, and is found, does God feel in welcoming the returning penitent to the arms of his eternal mercy. 'There is joy in the presence of the angels of God, over one sinner that repenteth.' "

Peace and joy now seemed to have taken up their abode under the roof of Mr. Howe. These parents have profited from their severe and bitter trial. Henry is no longer the marked favorite, but shares their love with his brother and sister. He too, is improved by suffering. He is never petulent, or impatient; for he remembers the real troubles that he was obliged silently to endure. He is always affectionate and obedient to his parents, for he recollects when no one gave him a kind word or look. He repays tenfold the love of his brother and sister, for he remembers the scoffing and unkindness which he used to receive from the children of his different tormentors.

He improves rapidly in his studies, and bids fair in every way to fulfil his early promise, and become a crown of rejoicing to his parents.